DRAGON'S REDEMPTION

DRAGON DREAMS 4

LEELA ASH

TABITHA ST. GEORGE

Join the Totally Romance Facebook Group!

https://www.totallyromancebooks.com/leela-ash

CONTENTS

*L*afferty's, the hottest restaurant in Jackson, Wyoming, boasted signature cocktails, aged steaks, and a Michelin star rating. Today, the entire establishment had been reserved for one purpose only.

To honor her.

Bree Williams surveyed the tables packed with tycoons and millionaires, the elite of one of the wealthiest cities in the US. They had come, decked out in their tuxedos and designer evening gowns, to toast her.

She deserved it. She'd made them all a hell of a lot of money.

Luxe Estates had just sold its last plot. Seventy-eight multi-million-dollar homes were about to be built. Elegant mansions with breathtaking views of the Grand Tetons.

How many challenges had she defeated? Well, to start with, six crotchety old ranchers, none of whom wanted to part with their land. Three zoning ordinances that had to be overturned. Four town meetings spent calming irate citizens who feared Luxe would be a glorified housing development.

And scores of title problems, each one a legal landmine that could sour the entire deal.

But she'd beaten those challenges, each and every one. Now she sat, surrounded by splendor, celebrated by the most powerful people in the state, on the verge of earning a seven-figure commission herself.

So why, she asked herself as she swirled her pisco sour, wasn't she happy?

The steak was perfect, the drink sharp and strong. The people were, well, a little tedious. Diamond-drowned elites trying to impress each other. Yet, the man at her side made up for that.

Daven Kane was her partner, the yang to her yin. A high-powered lawyer, the big gun she could always count on when negotiations failed. She sweet-talked the ranchers and smoothed the fur of the upset locals. He followed behind her. Slaying the legal problems she found. Making sure the contracts were tight and ironclad. And bringing out the knives whenever anyone tried to back out.

On top of that, he was good in bed. Lean, athletic, and willing to try anything once. Bree stole a sideways glance and admired his sharp cheek bones, the sweep of his dark hair, the way his eyes sparkled when he laughed. They were a great pair – both in bed and in the office.

So, why the melancholy?

She sipped her pisco, savoring the froth of egg whites that topped it. This always happened. She closed a deal, admirers laid the world at her feet… and instead of celebrating, she found herself like this. Staring into an expensive drink, wondering where her happiness fled.

"Don't like the drink?" Daven leaned close, surrounding her with the scent of his aftershave.

"Hmm? Oh, it's fine." Bree drew a deep breath, savoring the musky, masculine scent.

"Then why the long face? I hope it's not the company."

"No, no." She laughed and brushed his cheek with a light kiss. He waited, patient as always, until she shrugged. "I guess I'm just wondering what's next. What do I do now? Life seems empty without a project."

"Let me get this straight." His whisper was soft and warm against her ear. "Less than twenty-four hours after you close an enormous deal, and you're bored?"

"Not bored, no," she protested. "More like…"

"Hungry. Eager. Ready for the next challenge. That's what I love about you," he murmured as he nuzzled her hair. "I've never met a woman as ambitious as you. You're a natural born wolf."

High praise coming from him. Wasn't that what she'd always wanted? To be rich and powerful? To be a predator, not prey?

So, why this hollowness? This emptiness?

"Do you know what I need right now?" Bree slipped her foot out of her shoe and slid her stockinged foot along his leg.

Daven's smile sharpened, ravenous. "Right now…?"

"Yup. Right now, I need… another drink." Bree downed the rest of the pisco and waved her glass at the attentive waiter.

"Tease," he laughed.

"Well, I'll need other things later," she promised. "Just not in front of a crowd!"

The drink arrived. Then another. Then dessert (which, of course, had to be accompanied by a snifter of sherry). Then one more pisco for the road. As the speeches and toasts died out, Bree finally relaxed.

See? Enough alcohol always does the trick. Toss some good love-making on top of that, and everything will be fine.

Ting, ting!

Beside her, Daven rapped a knife against his wineglass, silencing the room with a bright, clear ring. "Ladies and gentlemen! I have one last announcement to make."

Pleasantly buzzed, Bree beamed at him as he rose to his feet. He gave her a quick nod then turned a radiant smile on the other diners. "We've spent the evening piling accolades on this magnificent woman. Now, with her consent, of course, I'd like to add one more."

Daven drew something out of his pocket and held it out before the crowd. Startled 'oohs' and 'aahs' swept across the room. She couldn't quite make out what this thing was, but clearly, people were impressed.

With a flourish, he turned and held out a tiny box. Nestled in its velvet-lined heart was a ring.

A ring with an enormous pea-sized diamond.

"I plan to make this lady Mrs. Bree Kane." Applause and cheers met his words.

People surged to their feet, clapping wildly. Only Bree remained seated, struggling to understand what was happening. Was Daven proposing? Normally, proposals involved questions not statements. But that was Daven for you. Questions gave people an opportunity to say 'no.' Better to stick to statements, right?

Could this be a joke? Bree swallowed and gazed up at him, trying to catch the glint of laughter in her lover's eyes. Unfortunately, she couldn't. Daven wasn't looking at her. His eyes swept the audience, drinking in their admiration and approval.

The diamond glittered, catching the table's candlelight and scattering it in a thousand gleams. Something that size must have set him back $100,000. It held her, dazed, like a deer in headlights. She couldn't bring herself to take it, though, and after a moment, the cheers wavered.

Only then did Daven look down at her, and his pleased expression dimmed. "Bree? You'll marry me, won't you?"

Would she? The urge to chug her pisco slammed her, hard.

Well, why shouldn't they marry? Daven was rich, handsome, and great in bed. He had ambition to match hers. What more could she ask for?

There was one obvious problem: love. Did she love Daven?

Honestly, it was kind of a stupid question. What was 'love' anyways? She liked him. A lot. They had fun together. Sure, idiots and hormone-crazed teenagers dreamed of something 'deeper.' Some eternal passion that would sweep them off their feet and dump them in a life-long paradise.

Adults knew no such thing existed. What she had with Daven was as good as it got. They'd be great together. A true power couple.

Besides, Bree thought, as she looked out over the sea of expectant faces, how could she reject him in front of Jackson's elite? It would be mortifying – for both her and him. And Daven wasn't the sort of man to let insults slide. If she publicly humiliated him, she'd turn her biggest ally into a life-long enemy.

Not the best reason for getting married, but hey! It's true. Might as well be realistic about this.

Even Daven had noticed her hesitation, and his bright, cheery smile drooped. Until she raised her glass.

"Sure! I mean, uh, yes. I do. I will. Or... whatever."

Laughter erupted around them and the applause rose once more. Grinning in triumph, Daven slipped the ring onto her finger.

"That is one impressive rock," she had to admit.

"Only the best for you!" He sank into his chair, nodding

thanks to his admirers. "You had me worried there for a minute."

"You surprised me." She twisted her hand back and forth in the candlelight. Half delighted, half embarrassed by the size of the diamond. This was *not* a subtle ring!

"Sorry about that. I've been thinking about it for a while."

Huh. She hadn't.

Not that Bree wanted to confess that.

"I thought we could aim for an October wedding," he continued.

Four months from now? "That's a little fast, isn't it?"

Daven shrugged. "Shouldn't be a problem. My secretary can whip a party together in a month. Plus, I've already drawn up a suggestion for the pre-nups."

Yeah, nothing said 'love' like a prenuptial agreement. Now, she did take a big gulp of her drink. Still, she couldn't blame him. No matter what people said, marriage wasn't really 'till death do us part.' It was more like, 'till boredom do us overtake.'

Yet, Bree remained unsettled. "A lot of people's event calendars will already be filled out, though. And October's kind of an off season. The summer residents are gone, and the skiers haven't arrived yet."

"Hmm. Good points," he admitted. "What about December? New Year's Eve, maybe?"

"Sure. We can steal the crowds away from the resorts."

He grinned at the challenge in her words and raised his whiskey to salute her. "New Year's it is, then."

"New Year's!" At least that bought her a couple more months.

Bree tapped her glass against Daven's and then downed the rest of her drink in one swallow.

. . .

THIS FAR NORTH, THE SUMMER SUN SET LATE. BREE LEANED her forehead against her Jaguar's steering wheel and cursed herself for a fool.

I'm drunk. Not falling down drunk, maybe, but bad enough to rack up a hell of a ticket if I got pulled over.

Why had she driven home? Why take that risk? She should have switched to water and stayed at Lafferty's for another hour or two.

With Daven and her agency.

Instead, she'd fled fifteen minutes after his proposal. The restaurant felt stuffy, close… and she needed to be alone.

Here. At home.

She loved this place. A luxurious log 'cabin', small by Jackson standards, surrounded by mountain meadows and patches of old pines. The obnoxious Mr. Nielsen, her only neighbor, was hidden behind an acre of trees.

Home at last, routine took her, and she found herself grabbing a bottle of wine to finish the evening, as she always did. Tonight, she put it back on the rack. More alcohol wouldn't clear her thoughts.

What she needed was the pool.

Her own personal retreat, the pool was a scrap of sanctuary from the world's cares. The little spring-fed pond had persuaded her to buy this place despite the fact that the house didn't have a good view of the Tetons.

Even in the evening gloom, her feet found the path easily. It was a trail of her own making, worn by her steps alone. Into the pines behind the house. Up a small hill and down the other side. Then straight through the cathedral-like arches of the grand Ponderosa pines until she reached the golden meadows along the edge of Rainey's Creek.

There, nestled among the wild grasses, lay a tiny pool, surrounded by worn stones and tall grass. Her secret spot. Fed by a strong artesian spring, its waters bubbled constantly. Clear and sparkling, they tasted almost sweet, as if eternal summer dwelled within the pool. A silver thread of glittering water wove through the grass, tying the pool to the creek.

Bree had never told anyone about this place. Never mentioned that when she sat there, her feet cooling in its crystal waters, all worries and cares vanished. Her mind became clear, sharp as a knife, and there was no problem she couldn't solve.

She still couldn't explain how she'd found the place. It wasn't on maps of the property. Neither the realtor nor its former owner had mentioned it. But the first time she set eyes on the woods, she'd been sure something important lurked in its depths. She'd left the realtor (still babbling about how, really, the lack of a Teton view wasn't *that* big of a downside) and followed her instincts. Along the route that would, in three years, become a path. And as soon as she saw the pool and its mysterious 'boiling' waters, she was sold. She paid full asking price for the property and never regretted it.

Now, once more, she traced the path to her sanctum, hoping it could work its charm on today's baffling events.

This time, however, when she stepped out of the woods, she wasn't alone.

A Dragon towered over her pool.

CHAPTER 2

*A*s he limped up the slow rise, one emotion dominated Finn Donnelly's thoughts.

Relief.

Thank God my Flight can't see me now.

For Heaven's sake, he hadn't even gone a quarter of a mile! Up a slope that he couldn't even call a hill. Yet, already, a dull soreness blossomed in his hip. A nagging ache that throbbed into true pain without warning.

Once more, he cursed the Witch Hare who'd stabbed him. Finn was a Dragon, the greatest warrior of the First Flight. There was no Shifter he wouldn't face gladly.

Except Witch Hares, damn them and their magic. Their sneaky, treacherous poisons and curses – one of the few things in this world that could actually harm a Dragon like him.

She was dead now, she and a Nest of Rats that served her. They'd been kidnapping Shifter children, forcing their families to serve the vile Fangs of Apophis. He'd rescued a dozen kids, all home with their parents now. But before he put that

Hare down, she left him one last gift. A three-inch scar on his left side that would not fully heal. Four months later, a walk in the woods left him limping.

It wasn't going to stop him, though. He had a job to do. Not a particularly interesting one, but a job was a job.

He needed to find a Wellspring.

Wellsprings were doorways between the worlds, gates that allowed the magical energies of the Other Side to flow freely. For centuries, they'd been closed, and the world grew cold and mundane. Then, three years ago, one awakened. Since then, his Flight had learned that love was the key to the Wellsprings. Left alone, they slept, dormant. Tended by a loving couple – by a Dragon and his Mate – they bloomed like desert flowers in the rain.

Now, the Dragons of his Flight warded a handful of Wellsprings, tiny beacons of hope in a tired world. His Alpha, Brandon Lorde, sent Finn here in hopes of finding another that could be fanned back to life by love's touch.

Somebody else's love, not his. He didn't have a Mate and didn't want one.

What he did have was the phone number of a Wolf pack in Montana. Once he found the Wellspring and acquired the land, he'd give them a call and turn it over to their protection. Wolves weren't as powerful as Dragons. But a Pack was a formidable foe, and with his Flight's backing, Finn was sure they'd be able to keep it safe from those who would exploit its magics. People like the Fangs.

First things first, though. He needed to ensure that there actually was a Wellspring here, as Lorde's research suggested.

And that was what had him limping up this sad little hillside and grumbling to himself.

A faint current ran through the air. A soft, invisible force that gently urged him to follow it. That was the call of the

Other Side. The Wellspring was close now. And healthy, judging from the strength of the draft.

Sure enough, his Shifter instincts brought him out of the woods less than fifty feet from the Wellspring. No surprises awaited him.

The first time he'd found a Wellspring, it set his heart racing. For one moment, he felt like a hero. As if he, alone, brought magic back and breathed life into this dull world. Six Wellsprings later, the excitement had faded. A little intuition, a little luck, a ton of hiking, and there you had it. Another Wellspring. Ready for someone else to fix.

This one looked like all the others. A charming pond half hidden by long meadow grasses. No signs of harm or damage. It was only a stone's throw from the edge of the property line, but that was fine. No neighbor would build a house this far back from the road. And the Wolves would love this place. Hell, they'd probably abandon the stodgy ranch down by the road and just camp out here, under the night skies.

Simple jobs were always a pleasure! Finn carefully measured the distance from Rainey's Creek to the Wellspring. As promised, the property line fell five feet beyond the spring. Good enough. Time to make an offer on Mr. Nielsen's property!

Movement along the wood's edge caught his eye.

Then a major problem stepped out of the forest.

A Witch Hare.

Tall and leggy, her brilliant red hair screamed she had a Witch's soul. Fate always seemed to bless Hares with beauty, and this one was no exception. Lithe and graceful, with the high cheeks of a noble lady and a rogue's full lips.

Whoever she was, she wasn't on his side. And she couldn't be alone – no Hare would challenge a Dragon directly! As he scanned the woods for her allies, Finn invoked his Shifter soul.

He grew, arms and body lengthening. Scales, thick enough to turn bullets, burst across his skin. Long scars crisscrossed them, mementos of battles past. His handsome, craggy face twisted into a fierce, fang-lined maw. A tail as long as a bus uncurled, and he reared back, spreading his wings wide.

A Dragon loomed where once a man had stood.

Finn tensed, expecting an ambush to burst forth. Yet, nothing happened.

The Witch Hare's jaw dropped… and then she closed her eyes.

What the hell? Finn sniffed, drawing in deep breaths. His keen senses found no hints of lurking Rats or fallen Wolves. Nothing but the scent of crushed grass and pine needles.

The woman opened her eyes. Blinked at him. Then closed them once again.

Details he'd missed suddenly popped into focus. She wore a little black dress, a skimpy, form-fitting piece of cloth that hid hardly any of her luscious curves. The 4-inch heels she clutched weren't made for hiking. In fact, her feet were clad in nothing more than stockings–now ruined.

Okay, that was *not* battle garb, even for a Witch.

Once more, the Hare opened her eyes. Finding him still there, she winced and peeked at him sideways, as if he might make more sense viewed from some other angle.

"What the hell did Daven put in my drink?" she hissed.

The odds of a fight seemed to be plummeting. With one last survey of the area, Finn dismissed his Dragon. Its majestic form faded away, leaving him human once again.

This seemed to calm the Hare, though she kept scrubbing at her eyes.

"Who are you?" he demanded.

At his imperious tone, she scowled. "Who am *I*? I'm the woman who owns this property. Who the hell are you and what are you doing on my land?"

"I am Finn Donnelly of the First Flight." If the Fangs had bought the land next door, he could have a major fight on his hands!

"Never heard of your company, mister. Why are you trespassing?"

To his shock, she seemed sincere. As if she'd never even heard of the world's most powerful Flight of Dragons.

Was she one of the Lost? Shifters who became cut off from their Kin as children and grew up never knowing what they were?

If so, that could explain why she wouldn't look at him straight on. Shifters recognized each other instantly. But if she'd never seen one...

She must feel like she's going mad.

Concentrating, Finn damped his power down as low as he could. His Dragon balked at the order. Roused by the threat of battle, the great serpent wasn't inclined to retreat. Despite its complaints, he dismissed it firmly.

Immediately, the blinking stopped. The Hare gulped and shook her head but grew calmer.

"I'm interested in buying the land of your neighbor, Lars Nielsen."

"Oh." Her nose wrinkled. Must be bad blood between the two of them. "Well, you've wandered off his property."

Wonderful. He had a Lost Hare camped on his Wellspring. "According to his deed, the property line runs to a point twenty feet west of Rainey's Creek. That would be," he pointed at the woods behind her, "ten feet into those trees."

"Wrong," she growled. Her Hare's ears folded down along its back and its little tuft of a tail jutted out stiffly.

Damn, Hares looked silly when they got mad!

"See, a landslide altered the course of Rainey's Creek about eighty years ago. It's now closer to my property than it was when the deeds were drawn. So, the true property line, as I've told Nielsen *several* times, is twenty feet that way. This spring," she jabbed a finger at the Wellspring, "is on *my* land."

"Property lines based on water features move as the water does."

"Not if the change is caused by avulsion rather than accretion." Her Hare took two short, aggressive hops toward him – and it was all he could do not to burst out laughing.

"I'll have to ask a lawyer what those words mean," he admitted.

"You do that. Best one in town is a good friend of mine. He'll also be the lawyer representing me if Nielsen decides to contest this."

Funny as her irate Hare was, the situation was quickly losing all humor. "Perhaps you'd be willing to sell the contested property? I'm happy to pay extra. I'm rather fond of this spring."

"So am I. And I don't intend to part with it."

She could probably sense the Wellspring's power, even if she didn't know what drew her to the site. This was turning into a right bloody mess. Finn made one last effort. "I'd be willing to pay…"

"Forget it." With a chop of her hand, she shut the conversation down. "Some things can't be bought. Good evening."

Without another word, she turned her back on him and started to stomp back the way she'd come.

"Ma'am? May I ask what your name is?"

"Bree Williams," she called over her shoulder.

"I'm Finn Donnelly. Look, we got off to a bad start. Maybe I could…"

The Hare gave no indication that she'd heard him. Just marched, bare-footed, into the gloomy woods.

Well, hell. What a mess.

CHAPTER 3

So much for stealing some quiet time to think! Caught between anger and fear, Bree peered into the mirror, searching for any damage to her eyes. A scratch... discoloration... anything that might explain why she was suddenly hallucinating. The alternatives – drugs slipped in her drink or madness – were even scarier.

What the hell is wrong with me? How could I make up a dragon?

The full vision hadn't lasted long. Yet, even once it disappeared, she couldn't look straight at that stranger. His form continually wavered, shifting between man and a gigantic beast with eyes of blue ice.

Something was wrong. Seriously wrong. She needed to see a doctor tomorrow, first thing.

And then Daven right after that. Fury melted the block of ice in her heart as she remembered her true problem. That pest, Nielsen, was trying to sell her land. *Her* pool!

Good thing her fiancé was a shark. As she slipped out of her dress and into a nightgown, Bree congratulated herself on tonight's choice. Marrying Daven was definitely the right thing to do.

In the dream, she stood in a prairie, waist-deep in golden grass. Blue sky arched overhead, cloudless and bright. A soft wind rustled through the field, setting the blades of grass whispering against each other. She wore nothing except a simple robe, tied over one shoulder like an ancient Greek dress. In her hands she held a silver goblet. A dragon with eyes of mother-of-pearl coiled around its stem.

It was a dream, clearly. Yet, so real that it took her breath away. She could feel the soil's cool damp against her bare feet, the way the sun warmed the skin on her arms.

From the grass ahead of her, a man suddenly yelped, "What the...?"

Finn Donnelly bolted to his feet.

Naked, apparently. Well, at least shirtless; the grass hid whatever he was (or wasn't) wearing below. Broad shoulders, bulging muscles, and a square jaw... boy, her subconscious wasn't sparing a single masculine trait. Now that he wasn't trying to steal her pool, she noticed other pleasant details. His blonde hair, cropped short in a no-nonsense buzz cut. His square jaw, Roman nose, and broad cheeks. And his eyes. Lord, what eyes that man had! Grey-blue, intense, like nothing she'd ever seen.

Bree informed herself that she approved of her taste in dream men.

His rippling muscles, gleaming in the sunlight, were criss-crossed with small scars that stood out white against his bronze skin. And as he gazed about him, his pale eyes filled with wonder and some dark, unreadable emotion.

"Oh hell," he whispered. "It's really happening. The Rite of Claiming."

Which made absolutely *no* sense. Then again, who expected sense from dreams?

As she pondered that question, an inhuman voice boomed in the clear sky, like the Voice of God. "No Claim without Truth. Show her your soul."

That sounded ominous. Bree waited... but nothing happened. Finn stood there, hands planted on his hips, staring out at the mountains.

"Ahem?" she prompted. "I think that thing was talking to you."

"I'm thinking."

"Okay." While she waited, she studied his powerful physique. Somebody worked out. A *lot*. And well. Chest, arms, abs, shoulders... not a single muscle group had been neglected. Her eyes kept drifting across the blonde curls on his chest, back to his shoulders. What would it feel like to be held in those arms, each one as large around as her calve?

Minutes passed. Bree found herself fidgeting. How the hell could a dream be this slow-moving? "So, uh, what's the hold up?"

"I'm *thinking*," he muttered.

"About...?"

"Whether or not I want to go through with this again." He turned to her, his blue-grey eyes burning with anger. "I don't believe in Fate. I make my own future. I won't be bound to a woman just because my Dragon thinks she's fine."

"Couldn't agree more," she assured him. Even though half of what he said didn't make any sense. "I really shouldn't have to interrogate the figments of my own imagination, but, well, here we are. Go through what? What's supposed to be happening here?"

"My Dragon wishes me to Claim a Mate. You."

Okay, so this *was* a sex dream. Good. She'd started to worry. "What does that involve?"

"I bare my soul. You do the same. Once we've looked upon each other with no illusions, we Claim each other. Symbolically, by dipping this dagger," he pointed at a small blade tied to his sash, "in your cup. Then physically, by making love. After that, we are bound together for all time."

Sounded good to her! The sooner they moved on to the hot sex, the better. "Well, no harm in the show 'n' tell, right? How do I show you my soul?"

"Call it."

"Um, right. Uh… here, soul," she crooned, feeling completely ridiculous. "Here soul-y, soul-y, soul."

Finn gaped at her like she'd lost her mind. But the grass at her feet rustled and a big, leggy rabbit hopped toward her.

Bree burst out laughing. "Oh, hell no, I'm not a bunny."

"That's a Hare, not a rabbit," he corrected. The animal's long ears plastered themselves against its back and it stared at her coldly.

"Bunny, hare, who cares? That's not me. I'm a wolf."

"No, you're a Witch Hare. They're powerful Shifters in their own way."

"Uh huh. Whatever." The hare stamped its hind foot in irritation. "There's probably some ridiculous, Freudian reason why I'd dream of being a useless rabbit, but I don't care. Get lost, Thumper."

With one more furious stomp, the Hare spun and bolted into the grass.

"Now, you."

Finn bowed his head and spread his arms wide.

The air behind him shimmered, filling with silvery light. Out of that glittering haze, an enormous figure came into view.

Despite herself, Bree took a step backward in shock. It was a Dragon. *The* Dragon. The one she'd hallucinated at the pool. As big as a small house, covered in creamy-white scales edged with bright silver. It's eyes… they were Finn's eyes. Pale grey orbs, like glacial ice, lit by some inner fire. Only, these eyes stared down at her from a sedan-sized head. One with a mouth full of six-inch fangs that would make a t-rex jealous.

Yet, after that moment of shock, joy flooded her. "It's… it's… beautiful!" she breathed. "Holy hell, I need a soul like that!"

With a snort that sounded like laughter, the Dragon faded from view, leaving an ache in Bree's heart. This dream was starting to look up.

"So, what's next? The cup and dagger thing?"

"*If* we wish to Claim each other."

"Well, I'm game." She eyed him up and down. "You're handsome, strong, and, well, a Dragon. What's not to like? I'll Claim you." And, most importantly, this was just a dream. Promises of eternal love would only last until morning.

Finn said nothing.

Seriously? The man of her dreams (literally…) was rejecting her? Damn, she needed therapy. "How about it? You going to Claim me?"

"I'm thinking."

"It was the bunny, wasn't it? I mean, who the hell wants to Claim a rabbit?"

"Hare. And no, it's not that."

"Is it me? Do you not like me?"

"No, I… It's me. I don't know if I can… if…." The sentence trailed off, unfinished. At last, though, he turned to face her. "I have failed so many times."

Bree stepped to him and put her hand on his elbow. This close, she could feel the warmth of his body. A heat that rose from him, summoning an equal fire deep within herself. "Nobody fails until they stop trying. So, what's you answer? Are you failing – or are you going to give this another shot?"

Even then, he hesitated, staring into the distance. Bree leaned closer, letting her bare thigh press against the taut lines of his muscles. At her touch, he tensed, and his breath quickened.

Good. No sign of any 'failure' here!

Back and forth he turned the blade in his hand, sunlight glinting off its edge. "Maybe you're right. I never Claimed anyone else."

Bree held her cup up, hopefully. With a worried grimace, Finn dipped the tip of his dagger into it.

At once, cup and knife both vanished. Bree's eyes lit up. "Fun part now?"

Finn released a deep chuckle, but he still seemed lost in thought. Normally, she didn't have to do much to seduce a guy. Yet, this was a dream (and a weird one at that) so she decided to take the lead.

The knot holding her robe in place proved delightfully simple to untie. One tug and the whole thing slid to the ground. Bree stretched, letting the sun set her tanned, golden skin alight, knowing damned well how it transformed her red hair into a brash, fiery crown.

Finn grew still. Eyes wide, he drank in the sight of her. Only his quickening breath and the pulse at his throat betrayed his mounting arousal. That control, that mastery, sent shivers of excitement down her spine. She needed to punch a hole through it, to reach the desire she knew burned beneath.

Slipping her arms around him, she snuggled closer. At the touch of her breasts, he tensed, and she felt his manhood stir. Her fingers traced the hard plains of his thighs and teased at his sash. She laid her head against his chest, listening as his beating heart hinted at the passion he held back.

Slowly, his arms circled her too, wrapping her in his heat. He bent his head, nuzzling her hair, until she tilted her head back. Then their lips met, softly at first, then firmer, more demanding as his hunger awoke.

When the kiss ended, he paused, lips parted. Some tension, locked deep within him, broke free and slowly drained from his face. Leaving him radiant, sure, and eager. "It has been so long…"

"Hope you haven't forgotten how this works…"

"Hmm. Was it something like this?"

He swept her off her feet as if she weighed no more than a kitten. Bree gave a shriek of delight as arms like steel bars cradled her. In daydreams, she'd longed to be carried off. To be taken, like a prize, to bed. No man had ever possessed the power to truly do it, though. Until now.

With an impish smile, he bent over her breasts. Kisses whispered across her skin and his tongue, with sly, teasing stokes, lashed her nipples.

A purr of pleasure escaped her. Instinctively, her back arched, offering her body to his mouth. Her hand caught at his short-clipped hair, pressing him close. Held, she surrendered to him and felt herself grow damp at the strange, vulnerable joy.

Slowly, he knelt, lowering her to the ground. But when the first blades of grass flicked across her bare skin, she burst into giggles. "Oh Finn, don't! That tickles."

"Hmm." He grimaced at the plains that spread around them. "That's going to be a problem. Maybe the woods?"

"Oh no. Pine needles are awful. And the pool is covered with rocks and mud."

"Not sexy," he said.

"Not sexy at all," she agreed. "Dammit! Work with me, dream!"

And the dream did! A sparkle of sun on bronze drew her eye to the middle of the field where a small platform covered in pillows lay amidst the long grasses. "Aha! Can I dream or what?"

Finn laughed and carried her to the bower with steady, sure strides.

Cradled against him, Bree felt a safety, a security, she'd never known. The power of this man, his strength, was the might of a Dragon, not a mortal.

Silken pillows, warmed by the sun, awaited them. Under the sun's brilliance, she noticed a web of white lines that crisscrossed his pale skin. She traced one with her finger, following it as it ran from his shoulder down his bicep.

"Gotten a bit beat up over the years," Finn admitted.

"I don't mind." To prove it, she pressed her lips to the scar and kissed it, reverently.

The sash around his hips slid off and was tossed into the grass. Once more, their mouths joined, lips and tongues twined in pleasure. Strong, calloused hands explored her body. Sliding across the smooth curves of her buttocks, exploring the cleft between her legs with soft, secretive caresses. Curled close, she felt his manhood swell as the scent and feel of her body brought him alive.

One hand came to rest between her legs, claiming her. Bree gasped at that touch, that heat, pressed against her most secret places. A finger slid between the damp lips of her sex. It found what it sought, the nub of her clitoris, and caressed it with firm, gliding strokes. A primal cry of need escaped her.

Her moans of pleasure, the way her body writhed beneath his touch… they enflamed him. His manhood swelled, pressing against her in its need. Yet, in the face of passion's maddening call, Finn was his own master.

Gently, he rolled over her. Muscled thighs slid between her legs and she opened herself to receive him.

His cock slid into her, filling her with its hard length.

Bree moaned, fingers knotting in the silken mounds of the cushions. With slow, sure strokes, he claimed her. Each thrust fanned the fires blazing in her loins. Raging, burning, her need grew. She moaned, wrapped her legs about his hips, and clawed at the pillows.

And still, those strokes continued. Hard, measured, maddening.

Bree wailed, an animal cry of desire. And at the sound, the first cracks appeared in Finn's control. His thrusts grew fiercer, hungrier, driven by her need. His own moans joined hers as they rocked, locked in the heat of passion.

Ecstasy blazed between her thighs. As she cried out, she felt him burst within her and his own guttural moan mingled with hers as he joined her in climax.

Gasping, he rolled to her side. Nestled in the cushions, Bree lay, panting, savoring the last traces of ecstasy as they faded away. "Damn," she whispered. "Why can't sex be this good in real life?"

Finn propped himself up on one elbow and kissed her shoulder. "It will be from now on. I promise."

"Yeah… no." She thought of Daven Kane and smiled. "Even in my dreams, my fiancé isn't this good."

"Your *what?*" Eyes blazing, Finn jerked away from her. "You have a… a…"

"Fiancé," she sighed. "And a wedding to plan for New Year's Eve."

"Why did you…"

AND BREE WOKE UP. WONDERING THE SAME THING.

Why did I dream of Finn when I'm going to marry Daven?

CHAPTER 4

The dream lingered long after Bree awoke. It haunted her in the shower, where every drop of water, trickling down her naked body, reminded her of Finn's tongue. It warmed her heart as she dressed and made her skip the loose, comfortable blouses she wore on her days off. No, today, she wanted something sexy. A skin-tight athletic shirt that made her curves sing. One with cleavage half-way down to her belly button. The kind of shirt that turned every man's head at the gym.

And when she polished off her morning smoothie, that dream was still there, casting a glow over the future. Yesterday, at the conclusion of the Luxe deal, the future had seemed a gloomy, empty mess. Today, there was a bounce in her step.

All because of a dream.

Sadly, it was a dream about a trespasser, not her fiancé.

That detail bugged Bree. The night of her proposal, she dreamed of making love to another man. A big, brawny guy who had absolutely nothing in common with her savvy lawyer.

I should make an appointment with a therapist. That can't be a good sign.

Later. After she took steps to protect her home.

First came a call to Jenna Magnuson, a private detective she sometimes used. "Hey, Jenna. Got a job for you. I want you to find out everything you can about a guy called 'Finn Donnelly'. Nope. No idea where he's from. The only thing I know is that he's in town and wants to buy the Nielsen property next door. Charge it to me, not the office. And cost isn't a concern."

Next up: another trip out to the pool. There ought to be stakes marking the property line. Something that didn't depend on the vagaries of Rainey's Creek. Bree had never found them. Then again, she hadn't looked hard.

Time to change that. No way she'd let that scum ball Nielsen steal her pool.

To Bree, the short path to the pool was the most beautiful walk in all of Jackson. But today...

Today, it was magical. Every breath of air she drew was rich with the lovely scent of pine and grass. Birds flittered on all sides, filling the woods with their songs. Beams of sunlight pierced the tree cover, lighting her path with golden pillars. There was a crispness to the air, an energy, as if some great storm had just passed.

When she emerged beside the pool, she gasped. The spring's water glittered in the sun like a thousand diamonds. Everything seemed brighter, from the tufts of grass to the glint of Rainey's Creek in the distance.

Clearly, I need more dreams like last night's!

Bree laughed, giddy with joy. Not even the fear of losing the little pool could dim her excitement.

Though, as soon as she walked out into the meadow, she realized this was a lost cause. The field wasn't huge, probably no more than ten acres. Yet, it was covered in thick, luxurious grass. Somewhere, hidden beneath all this wonder, was one lone solitary stake.

How could she possibly find it?

Bree nibbled her lip. Metal detector? Realtors used metal stakes that wouldn't rot as the years passed. She could pop into town, buy one, and spend a day or two sweeping this area.

Or...

She could trust her gut. Bree considered instinct one of her greatest strengths. Over the years, her hunches had uncovered lying clients, falsified deeds, and a host of other deceits. She always knew how far to push negotiations and when a client couldn't live without a property.

So, why not give luck a shot? At worst, she'd waste five minutes.

Bree closed her eyes, tilting her face back and letting the sunlight pour down around her. She threw her arms wide, like Finn had in her dream. Then, blind, she began to inch forward.

Something tugged at her. An urge, a phantom nudge. It pulled her to the right, slowly cutting an arc through the grass. Her heel landed on a gopher hole. She wobbled but refused to open her eyes. One more step, two... and then her foot struck something hard.

Dropping to her knees, she swept the long grass aside. There, driven deep into the soft earth, was what she sought: a property stake.

Proving that the pool belonged to her, not Nielsen.

"Ha!" Bree crowed. "Score one for Witch Bunnies!"

Quickly, she flattened down the surrounding grass. It wouldn't stay bent for long, but a picture showing the distance between the stake and the pool would save her a ton of legal research.

She raised her cell phone... and froze.

Behind her, the pool had vanished.

In its place stood a patch of mist, thick as cotton. On some cool mornings, wisps of mist danced above the pool's swirling waters. But never anything like this. Nothing so deep and foreboding. And sudden! Where on Earth had it come from?

Wary, she crept back toward it. Crazy theories popped into her head. Had she been wrong about the pool all along? Was it actually a thermal hot spring? One that was becoming more active?

Nonsense. Hot springs are hot. *Duh. The pool has always been ice cold.*

Still, she was cautious as she approached. Twisted in a knot, her gut warned her that something was wrong.

Something was *dangerous.*

As the mist swallowed her, all noise died away. The birds, the squirrels, the crickets in the field... all faded. Not even the pool's never ending gurgle cut through the silence. Only her ragged breathing still echoed in her ears.

Hairs on her arms prickling, she inched forward, careful not to slip on the mossy stones.

Wait. *Mossy* stones?

The pool was surrounded by waist-tall grass, not rocks! Shivers swept over her and her heart raced. What had happened? No one could have crept up behind her and mowed the field without her knowing. That was insane!

Out of the corner of her eye, she saw movement. A figure, tall and impossibly thin.

Bree snapped around toward it – and it vanished.

More forms appeared in the periphery. Vague phantoms that faded away as soon as she turned toward them. Whispers echoed through the mist. Soft voices speaking in a lilting, musical language she didn't understand.

There were creatures here. No, she corrected herself.

People. A dozen of them, or more. Watching her. Melting away at the edge of her vision.

Fear rose. She turned to flee…

"Hold."

A woman's voice – or had she imagined it? Bree hesitated. Fear urged her to flee. Yet, the yearning in that strange voice held her in place.

"Your… mixing." Wonder and longing. The words ached with them. "It is beautiful. Light and dark. Spirit and body. You are…"

As if a cloud had passed in front of the sun, the mist darkened. Cold air, dank and frigid, rose from the ground and chilled her feet. The whispers shot away, as if her invisible audience had all turned and fled.

A shadow loomed. The dark twin to the misty ghosts that had flitted at the edges of her vision.

Unlike them, this thing was cold. And it didn't vanish when she stared at it. It grew stronger, clearer. Hate and revulsion radiated from it.

Eyes wide, Bree backed away.

From the darkness, a man's voice hissed. "You are unclean. Leave."

Bree didn't need to be told twice. She spun on her heels and bolted for home. Stones, slick and damp, skittered underfoot. Then grass whipped against her hands and pelting feet. Grass gave way to pine needles, a tree loomed in the mist… then her foot caught on a root and she when sprawling onto the forest's soft floor.

With a soft shriek, she spun, fearing that the dark figure pursued her.

The mist was gone. She lay at the edge of the woods, staring out at a clear, sunny meadow. Once more, the pool's musical waters called.

Bree ignored them. She scrambled to her feet and ran all the way home.

CHAPTER 5

"Well, I hope you're happy," Finn told his Dragon.

Utter devastation spread in all directions around him. Two-foot trenches clawed in the Earth. Uprooted trees, their wood shattered into matchsticks. Even a handful of boulders with large chunks gouged out.

That was his work. Or, rather, his Dragon's.

He'd awakened from Bree's…

…treachery!…

…Bree's shocking confession, he corrected his Dragon. Furious, swimming in rage. Dragon's didn't handle…

…treachery!…

…disappointment well. 'A true Dragon is his own master', as his Alpha was fond of saying. Yet, it was also true that a wise man picked his fights. Maybe he could force his wild soul to swallow its pride. But why bother? Better to fly out here, far from civilization, where it could vent its rage safely. A few squirrels might die of fright, but that was the worst of it. This mess? A feast for beavers and woodpeckers.

Now, with the red rage finally dimming, he sat down amidst the ruin and tried to think.

So much for 'true love.' His 'soul mate' was promised to another man.

That admission stung, a sharp, stabbing blow to the heart that set his Dragon's fury flaring again.

"I am such an idiot," he said to no one. "This time, this time, things would be different. Hah."

She is a traitor!

"No." Firmly, he pushed his Dragon's rage out of his mind. "She's one of the Lost. Probably never Shifted in her entire life. She has no idea what the Rite of Claiming is. To her, this was just a strange dream. Of course, she didn't take it seriously!"

But he had. For one night, for one glorious moment, he had dared to believe…

He cut that thought off too. He'd dared to believe stupid things. Best not to dwell on that.

Not when he needed to plan for the future.

Clearly, Bree Williams was not his woman.

We Claimed her! his Dragon protested.

"Oh, great! She's a traitor but we Claimed her, so… what? She's *our* traitor? Nobody else can have 'our' traitor?"

Fuming, his Dragon refused to answer.

The first prick of a headache blossomed behind his eyes.

He would die of shame if his Alpha, his Flight, found out how he'd been humiliated. He could never mention that stupid dream. On that, he and his Dragon agreed.

"So, we're going to let her go."

His Dragon seethed.

"Stop it. If we can't love her, we're letting her go to a man who can. She deserves love, if she can find it."

There. That quieted his soul.

"We never mention this." Again, embarrassed agreement.

"We do our job, buy this Wellspring, and call the Wolves in to care for it. Then we leave."

And this humiliation would be just another failing in a long, long list.

An urge welled up inside him. He longed to Shift once more and vent his anger on the land around him.

But he wouldn't. Enough was enough.

Time to fly back to Jackson. Time to put 'love' and all of its horrors behind him once more.

CHAPTER 6

omething followed her back.

Bree saw it out of the corner of her eye. Hazy forms in doorways that disappeared as soon as she faced them. Movements she caught out of the corner of her eyes. She heard it. Whispers in the night. Footsteps in empty rooms. Night after night, she dreamed of the pool, lost in the mist.

Home didn't feel safe anymore.

On Monday morning, after a sleepless weekend, Bree broke down and called her therapist, who promptly pointed out the obvious: this was just stress. Closing a huge deal, getting engaged... no wonder her nerves were shot! Fortunately, the therapist assured her, there were drugs to take care of things like this. One quick consultation and he'd write her a prescription.

In the meantime, he recommended meditation and yoga.

Right. Bree almost laughed as she made the appointment. Like she was going to sit still that long!

No, what she needed was to get out. Away from the

silence and solitude. A few hours in town, in the middle of life and fun, would do wonders.

Downtown Jackson boasted scores of shops, ranging from tourist kitsch to designer chic. Everything a budding millionaire could want. Bree spent a couple hours window shopping. Surrounded by noisy, happy people, she felt her spirits rise. Just as she'd hoped, the bustle of humanity warmed her.

By noon, she had a healthy appetite and headed over to Lafferty's. No fast food for this lady! The waiter whisked her to her favorite table in the back, one that overlooked the restaurant's courtyard garden. They passed Daven, listening attentively as an older woman prattled about trusts and funds and irresponsible grandchildren. Her fiancé gave a little wave but never took his eyes off his client.

Just as she expected. Business came first. And it was just as well. A courier delivered the pre-nups on Saturday. Daven would want to know if she consented to them, so the wedding could move ahead. Bree didn't want to admit that, despite the fact that absolutely nothing had happened, she hadn't found the time to look them over.

Settled in her favorite spot, sipping on a glass of a California merlot, she started to feel like herself again.

Until he walked in.

Finn Donnelly.

Like a shark drifting through a school of minnows, he glided through the restaurant. A tantalizing hint of danger lingered around his big, powerful form. The men he passed seemed to shrink, to dwindle, dwarfed by his broad size. A white polo shirt clung to his muscled form. Its short sleeves revealed his biceps for the admiration of all the women here.

Bree remembered those arms. Her body warmed as she recalled how they wrapped around her, claiming her, lifting her into...

...something that didn't *happen!*

With a sigh, she gazed out the window. How embarrassing! To be mooning about a dream in public. Worse – in front of her fiancé! Therapy and drugs couldn't happen fast enough!

When she looked back, she found him staring at her.

Anger lit his grey-blue eyes. Teeth clenched, lip pulled back in a half snarl, he was the picture of barely restrained rage. What the hell was *he* mad about?

Bree glared back. She'd show him she couldn't be intimidated!

"Mr. Donnelly! How good to see you." His eyes narrowed as he stalked over to her table. "Won't you join me?"

"I'd rather not."

Sharp, cold, and menacing. Nothing like his friendly demeanor the other day. What on Earth had Nielsen told him? Something about her, obviously. Something awful.

One again, the ghostly image of a Dragon shimmered behind him. When she blinked, it was gone. Another quiet warning that she needed to see that therapist, soon.

"Please." She waved at the empty seat. "It's about the property line."

Wary, he took the seat and folded his arms across his broad chest. Classic hostile body posture, she noted. "I'm having a title search done on your neighbor's property. That should clear up any questions about the property line."

"I can save you the trouble. I found the property markers in the middle of that field. They prove that the pool is on my land, not my neighbor's."

"You'll forgive me if I do my own research. You're not exactly trustworthy, are you?" His rich, deep bass rumbled like a bear's warning growl.

"Excuse me?" Bree leaned forward, refusing to be cowed. "Have I done anything to you? No."

Finn took a deep breath, as if he planned to disagree. Then his mouth snapped shut.

"I don't know what stories my neighbor told you. Yeah, there's bad blood between us. Maybe some of it's my fault. But who cares? Honestly, I'd like to see you buy his place. It would get him out of my hair. Don't let him poison our relationship."

"Our relationship." He winced, like he'd bitten tin foil.

Damn, he was a strange man! Still, she might end up living next to the weirdo. Best to smooth things over if she could. "Look, if you have concerns, tell me. I want us to be good neighbors."

The wrath that lit his face dimmed. As it did, his shoulders sagged, as if anger had been the only thing holding him up. "I apologize. I'm just annoyed. I was very fond of that little pool. I could offer you money – a lot of money – to sell it to me. But obviously, you're not interested."

Of course not.

Was she?

Friday, she would have said no. *Hell* no. After a haunted weekend, though? After eerie mists, ghostly figures, and an empty house that seemed filled with invisible people?

"Probably not." Even to her ears, that sounded more like a question than a statement.

Finn straightened, instantly alert. "Are you suggesting that you might sell?"

"No promises. I just… I've been thinking of selling my house. Moving into town where things are livelier. It gets a little lonely out there."

"I would, of course, be happy to purchase your home instead of your neighbor's."

Wow. Fixate much? "I'm not sure, of course. I need to think about this more." And see if therapy, drugs, and a spa day fixed her 'stress' problem.

That announcement should have made him happy. Instead, he leaned toward her. The last traces of hostility melted away from his craggy face. "It's none of my business, Ms. Williams, but has something happened?"

"No. Why do you ask?"

"Because three days ago, you were ready to challenge me to a duel – just because I had the audacity to want your land. Now, you say you might sell. What changed?"

"I... Nothing." An annoying little quaver trembled in those words.

"You can tell me." His hands, rough and warm, closed around hers. Hands she'd dreamed caressed her body, stroking her...

Bree gulped, struggling to focus on reality. "Nothing. Honest. Nothing happened, not really."

She ought to pull away from him. Pretty cheeky of him to scoop her hands up like this. They didn't even know each other! Yet, a reassuring strength lay in his hands and Bree found herself unwilling to leave it.

"Tell me, please." Pale eyes, clear as ice, bore into hers. Yet, his tone was gentle. Like a cowboy calming a skittish colt. "I will believe you. No matter how crazy your story may be."

Tempting. So tempting. But...

"Pardon me."

Daven stood by their table, scowling at her.

Why was *he*... oh! Bree's cheeks blazed as she realized she was still holding Finn's hands. Quickly, she pulled them away and folded them in her lap.

Finn glanced at the newcomer – and immediately, anger lit his face once again. "Ah. The fiancé," he sneered.

How did he know she was engaged? She'd dreamed she told him – but it hadn't really happened!

Not that she had to say anything, she realized suddenly.

She wore a rock the size of Mt. Everest and Daven was definitely giving off a 'PO'd Boyfriend' vibe.

"Daven! This is Finn Donnelly. He's interested in buying the Nielsen property."

"Really?" Her fiancé inched closer to Finn, towering over the seated man. "And so, the two of you decided to… have lunch?"

"No. Ms. Williams called me over to let me know she'd found the property markers. There was some confusion."

"Was there?" Daven stared pointedly at the other man's hand, which had so recently enclosed hers.

Finn rose to his feet. Now, *he* towered over Daven by six inches. "Yes."

Nervously, the lawyer scuttled back, putting a little distance between them.

Bree knew she should diffuse the malice simmering between the two men, but the whole situation baffled her. She didn't understand Finn's anger, or the reason he scooped up her hands. Or why she hadn't repulsed him the moment he did.

Finn pulled a business card out of his wallet and set it in the middle of the table. "My number, Ms. Williams. Please do call me if you decide to sell your property."

With a nod to her and to Daven, he walked out.

Her fiancé recovered his courage as soon as the big man turned away. Glaring at Finn's back, he sat down across from her and took her hands in his.

Something he never did.

Without thinking, she pulled away – and immediately realized that was a mistake when Daven's scowl turned on her.

"Are you okay?"

"Of course!" Bree gave a short, fake laugh to reassure him.

"I just wanted to clear up the property line confusion and save myself some legal fees."

"I wouldn't *ever* charge you. I'll defend you for free if he bothers you again!"

Offers of protection ought to be charming – but this one left her cold. It was too silly, too angry. Daven reminded her of a dog barking furiously because another dog had peed in his yard.

That's unkind. He's just doing this because he loves you.

Really? Then why he was scowling at her like she was the villain here?

"When did you plan to tell me about your move?" His lips pinched in a thin, hostile line.

"My what? Oh! I don't intend to move. I just want to keep my options open."

"I could see that," he sneered.

That was the last straw. Her own temper rose to match his. "What do you mean by that?"

"You know what I mean."

She did. But she wanted to force him to admit it. "Are you saying I'm not allowed to talk to other men now that we're engaged? That's going to shoot my career in the head."

"That's not what I'm saying at all."

"Then what *are* you saying?"

"I'm saying we're a partnership now and you need to start running things like this by me before you do them."

Their first argument. Wonderful. Was this what she had to look forward to in their marriage? "Things like what? What do you think happened here?"

"You planning to move."

Damn, that pout made her want to slap him! Bree turned away before the urge grew stronger. As she did, she spotted a large black puddle by Lafferty's front door. A slick, black pool, as if someone had dribbled car oil all across the fancy restaurant.

"Well?"

"Well, what?" Daven's angry question drew her attention away from the mess.

"Are you going to apologize?" That pout was back, in full force.

"For what? For thinking I might possibly move?"

"For not including me."

"In *what*? In my thoughts?"

Oh, this was ridiculous. Bree shook her head, furious, and…

The puddle was gone.

No, not gone. *Moved.* Now it pooled in the aisle halfway to their table. As she watched, a waiter whisked through it, dirty dishes balanced on his arms. Nothing happened. He didn't slip. The puddle didn't ripple. Nothing dirty got tracked across the floor.

A shadow? No, it was too dark, its edges too sharp. Staring at its inky, unmoving surface, Bree shivered.

"Yes, in your thoughts," Daven hissed. The lawyer was vibrating with quiet fury but still tried to keep his voice low. Mustn't cause a scene in public, after all! "If you're thinking about making a major life change, you need to…"

"Stop." She tapped him on the hand, silencing his complaints. Suddenly, she couldn't care less about this idiotic fight. "What's that?"

She pointed at the aisle.

The clean, spotless aisle…

Daven turned, grumbling, "What's what?"

It was gone again.

Or was it?

Bree's blood turned to ice. Slowly, knowing what she was going to find, she looked down.

A puddle of purest midnight pooled around their feet.

With a shriek that turned every head in the place, she snatched her feet up onto her chair.

"Bree!" Shock wiped the pout off his face. "What the hell is wrong with you?"

"Don't touch it! Daven, move your feet move…"

And, of course, he didn't listen. He ducked his head under the table but left his feet planted firmly in the middle of that horrible blob. "Don't touch what?"

"*That!*" She jabbed a finger at the mess he sat in.

"I don't see anything. Was there a mouse?"

A mouse? Bree's head snapped up but there was no sign of sarcasm in his face. Puzzled, he stared down at his feet.

And saw nothing.

No puddle. No ink. No shadowy menace creeping across the floor.

What is wrong with me? I better head over to the therapist's now. *Appointments be damned, this is an emergency.*

Of course, when she looked down again, it was gone. Completely.

She was nuts. Crazy. Bonkers.

Fortunately, her fiancé *had* offered her a way to salvage her pride. "Yeah, a mouse. I saw a…"

Daven's hand slammed down upon her wrist. Fingers like iron cables closed, holding her hand in an unbreakable grip. "Ow! Daven, what the hell?"

The man who glared at her from across the table wasn't Daven.

Oh, he wore Daven's body, that lean, handsome form she knew so well. But his eyes…

His eyes were pure black. Two tiny pools of darkness.

"This is your 'love'?" Contempt dripped from each word. Daven's lips curled with revulsion, as if he held a slimy worm instead of his fiancée's hand. "This is the 'miracle' of which your kind boasts?"

"Daven, let go. You're hurting me." She tried to jerk free, but her hand seemed nailed in place.

"Rage. Jealousy. Pettiness. Greed." Each word spat out like a piece of filth. With each, his voice rose. Heads turned, waiters froze. Every eye in the place was fixed on them.

"Daven..."

"He rots under your touch," the creature sneered. "The darkest parts of his soul grow strong. The light dies. Because of you. Your 'love' is filth, manure that you vomit on a soul, polluting it with..."

With a crack like the blast of a shotgun, the door to the restaurant slammed open. Through it barreled a welcome sight.

Finn Donnelly.

The big man plowed through the restaurant at a dead sprint. Tables, patrons, waiters... anything in his way got shoved aside. How could someone so large move that fast? Nothing slowed him. He bolted across the room, straight to her table.

He slammed his hand down on Daven's arm, pinning it in place. No doubt. No hesitation. No flinching.

"Let go of her."

Finn didn't yell. He didn't need to. Rage vibrated in each word, a fierce, protective fury.

For her. He was protecting *her*. Shock and relief warred in her heart. No one – not family or boyfriend – had ever stood up for her like this.

Yet, Daven's hand remained locked on her wrist. Disgust radiated from those dead black eyes.

"Let go of her or I break your arm," Finn clarified.

Her fiancé's nose wrinkled with annoyance. Then he blinked, blinked again... and his eyes cleared. Revulsion vanished, replaced by horror. "Oh, Bree! Bree! I'm so sorry! I don't…"

As Finn released him, he clamped his hands over his mouth. Her savior took a step back but hovered close, ready to pounce at the first sign of a threat.

Bruises lined her wrist. One for each of Daven's fingers. "What the *hell* is wrong with you?" Her voice carried in the silent restaurant. Every pair of eyes were fixed on them and the incident.

"I don't know. I don't know why I…"

He reached for her – but not as fast as Finn. The big man's hand snapped out and caught Daven's halfway across the table. "Don't touch her."

"It's not my fault! I don't know what happened to me!"

Finn's lip curled at that feeble excuse.

But Bree believed him. She'd seen that shadow – and that thing, whatever it was, that glared at her out of her fiancé's eyes.

Not that anyone would believe her. Shaking, she wobbled to her feet. Instinctively, Finn caught her elbow and steadied her. Gallant, even in the middle of a confrontation.

"I'm leaving, Daven. We'll talk later."

On unsteady feet, she walked away from the trembling man. Finn followed her, keeping himself between her and Daven at all times. As they passed the *maître de'*, he produced a couple of hundred dollar bills. "For the mess. My apologies."

Outside, in the sunlight and fresh air, her fear receded, like a bad dream. Bree wrapped her arms around herself, letting the bustle of life drive away the chill. Finn waited patiently, watching.

"Thank you," she said when she finally stopped trembling.

"You're welcome."

What she wouldn't give to throw herself in his arms! To let him hold her, promise her everything would be all right.

She didn't do that, of course. And he didn't invite it, either. Cool and guarded, he kept his distance. More like a bodyguard than a savior.

"Are you going to be all right?"

"Yes, I'll be fine. I…" What could she say? The whole situation was mad.

"Thanks. Thanks again." Lord, that was lame. But how could she explain how he'd made her feel? To know that a man would defend her, violently if needed. To feel his steady strength, his rock solid courage, backing her up?

"As I said, you're welcome." Not a drop of kindness warmed his words. He was cool, polite, and formal.

Head bowed, Bree turned and headed for her car. Leaving her feelings unspoken.

And Finn let her go.

CHAPTER 7

The Skyline Lodge was designed for relaxation. From the soft pastels of its walls to the luxurious carpet underfoot, every detail urged its guests to forget the worries of the outside world. Kick your shoes off. Hop in the hot tub. Pop open a cold one and just **relax!**

Finn wasn't having any of that. Back and forth he paced, ignoring the breathtaking Teton view just outside his window.

Daven Kane was a worm. A slimy, cowardly, craven worm.

And that worm had stolen *his* Mate!

Livid with fury, his Dragon raged inside his mind.

We should have driven that thief off!

"I doubt that would have impressed Ms. Williams."

It would have shown her how weak he is! He is not worthy of her!

Couldn't disagree with that. But what his Dragon couldn't accept was that it didn't matter. Bree got to choose. And if she chose the worst man…

…She'll be like every other woman I've ever thought I loved.

No, that wasn't fair. Some of them were good women.

Women he'd failed to protect.

The memory of those disasters dimmed his Dragon's outrage. Though, it still stewed.

We should lie out in the sun. Let her see our might and how the sun gleams upon our scales. Then she would choose differently.

Finn snorted with laughter. Oddly put, but his Dragon had something of a point. There were other ways to fight. Ways that didn't involve beating the other guy to a pulp and carrying the woman off like a prized chunk of meat.

If he cared to fight for her. Which he didn't.

The bottom line still remained: he didn't *want* a Mate. Which made going through with the Rite of Claiming even more idiotic. He must have fallen prey to a bout of temporary insanity. That, or he let himself get seduced by Bree's hot, tanned body. In either case, he'd screwed things up. Again. 'Real' or not, the Rite created a powerful link between the two of them.

The incident at Lafferty's proved it. A Dragon always knew when his Mate was in danger. That's what the stories said, anyways. Finn never believed them. He'd loved a dozen women in his long years and not once had he felt a supernatural urge to protect them.

Until today.

Until it hit him as he waited for a taxi. A burning certainty, a dread that drove his Dragon berserk in a heartbeat.

His Mate was in danger.

He knew where she was. How, he couldn't say. But when that horror settled on his soul, he found himself sprinting through traffic, ignoring screaming brakes and blaring horns. The wound in his hip that had dogged him for months? Gone, completely, as if it had never happened. He tore through downtown Jackson at full speed, running as if his life depended on it.

Because it did. *Her* life depended on it and he knew, with a Dragon's fierce passion, that he'd die before he let anything harm her.

Bree Williams truly was his Mate. The other half of his soul.

And she'd chosen someone else.

The buzz of his cell phone broke through that gloomy thought. A foolish hope flickered through his heart. Was it her? Would she call him back? Then he recognized the number and that ridiculous hope died.

Brandon Lorde. His Alpha.

"Good afternoon, Lorde." The man might be his Alpha, but all Dragons were fierce, proud creatures. There would be no titles or signs of submission between them.

"Donnelly. I may need to recall you. Be ready to leave at a moment's notice."

"What's wrong?" Even as he spoke, Finn strode to his closet and snatched his shirts off their hooks. To him, 'a moment's notice' meant 'be ready NOW.'

Grim yet calm, Lorde gave him the worst news possible: "The Wellsprings are fading."

"How?" he barked. "They're supposed to be protected!"

"They are. Even mine is failing."

That stopped him in his tracks. If the Alpha of the First Flight couldn't protect a Wellspring, what hope was there?

"We don't know what's causing this. It started a couple days ago and it's accelerating rapidly. At this rate, they'll all be dormant again within the month."

And just like that, all their hope would vanish. The Rite of Claiming… magic… his Flight's renewed vigor and sense of purpose… all would be gone.

Finn pushed that weak thought aside. Nobody was giving up.

Especially not his Alpha. "Darian Morland and his Mate, Tess, are here now. She may be able to give us some unique insight into the cause."

Tess Morland was some weird type of Shifter. An 'Adanai' or something like that. Finn was a little vague on the details. Normally, he just wrote her off as a strange Witch Hare.

"Is there anything I can do?" Magic wasn't his strong suit, but he couldn't stand to be useless.

"At the moment, no. When we uncover the cause, I may need you."

"I'll be ready," he promised.

There was a pause, long and awkward. The kind of silence that often popped up when two men weren't good at small talk. "Things progressing well in Wyoming?"

"Yes."

A lie. But he wasn't going to confess how horribly wrong things had actually gone. To admit that you found – and *lost* – a Mate… to a nothing like Daven Kane…

No. He couldn't do that. The shame would destroy him.

"Good. How's the hip?"

"Good." Surprisingly good, now that he thought about it. His little sprint through downtown Jackson hadn't hurt at all. If anything, he felt better!

"Glad to hear it." More silence. "Well, I'll call if you're needed."

"And I'll be ready," Finn promised.

CHAPTER 8

With the TV blasting at full volume, Bree almost missed the doorbell. Quickly, she clicked off the set and peered through her peephole. Her stomach, roiled by the unexpected bell, settled as she recognized a delivery man from Flowers By Dana.

In his arms he held a dozen red roses, nestled in a crystal vase. *Real* crystal. Waterford, by the looks of it. Trust Daven not to skimp on any expense.

"Delivery for Ms. Bree Williams."

"Thank you." She took the form from him and signed.

"Where should I put them?"

"I'll take them."

She held her hands out for the bouquet, but he shook his head. "Lady, there's a bunch more."

She pointed him to the kitchen table. He deposited his burden. Then another… and another… and another. By the time he was finished, twelve dozen roses graced her kitchen. Each one perfect. Each one held by its own $100 vase.

"Somebody loves you," the delivery man grinned as he dumped the last of these beauties.

That did seem to be the message behind this display.

Be nice. Flowers are a lovely way to apologize.

True. Yet, every time Daven showed his 'feelings' for her, she ended up marveling at the price tag, not his sincerity.

Though, she reminded herself, he *had* called. Four times. Swearing up and down that he had no idea what came over him at Lafferty's. Begging her to forgive him, to give him another chance.

She'd agreed. Of course.

Because something *had* come over him, literally. And whatever it was, it followed her home.

When the delivery man arrived, it hid. But as the door closed behind him, the whispers came slithering back. Louder now, as if the flowers riled her unseen guests.

Quickly, she clicked the TV on. Once more, its incessant blare drowned out those other, more frightening sounds.

What the hell was she going to do? Sick with fear, Bree stared at the flowers. Flickers of white, like pale ghosts, flitted among them.

A sane woman would flee to her therapist. That's certainly what she had planned to do.

Until today. Until lunch.

Now, she knew she wasn't mad. Madness wasn't contagious. She couldn't infect Daven and make him assault her. His eyes and his crazy behavior were evidence that the world was mad – not her.

Which brought her back to the same old question. What now?

Curled up on her couch, with only the idiot noise of the TV between her and the ghosts, Bree decided to do the only sensible thing.

Get out.

. . .

"I must admit, I'm surprised, Ms. Williams."

Perched awkwardly on top of one of her delicate kitchen stools, Finn's square bulk was wonderfully calming. Her ghosts seemed to find him even scarier than the delivery man. The moment he walked through the door, her home returned to its own normal self.

"I'm not indecisive," she said. "I thought about your generous offer and decided to sell."

"Well, I won't argue. What's your price?"

She named a high figure. True to his word, he quadrupled it.

"Seriously?" Wealthy as she was, that extravagance still made her head spin.

"Yup. There's only one condition."

Ah, but of course. The deal was too good to be true. "And what would this 'condition' be?"

He leaned toward her. Intent, focused, and somber. "You have to tell me what's wrong."

"Wrong?" She laughed nervously. "Nothing's wrong."

Those intense blue-grey eyes ignored her lies. "Nobody changes their mind this quickly."

"Look, if you're worried there's something wrong with the house, the inspection will turn up any…"

He dismissed that with a sharp wave of his hand. "It's you I'm concerned about, not the house. You're afraid. Why?"

"Don't be silly!" Her giggles sounded hollow, even to her. They had *no* chance of deceiving Finn.

"You seem to think you're in danger… but you're not."

Okay, that annoyed her. "Oh, I'm not? And how exactly would you know that?" Just like a man, to presume he knew everything!

"I would, actually." A glint of humor lit his serious eyes. "But since you're not being honest with me, I'm not going to explain how."

Whatever. Tonight, she wasn't in the mood for either him *or* Daven. "Look, do you want this house or not?"

"Yes. But I want the truth too." Suddenly, his eyes widened. He straightened, nearly tipping the little stool over. "Hang on. This thing… whatever it is that's got you spooked. Did it start Saturday? Maybe out by that little pond we argued over?"

Bree's jaw dropped. "How on Earth did you know that?"

"Ha!" He hopped to his feet, sparing her stool from further menaces. "Because there are a lot of other places like your spring. And they all started having 'issues' two days ago."

Her thoughts reeled. Was there really a sane explanation for all of this madness? "Wait. Is the pool, like, volcanic or something? Is it giving off a gas?"

"Gas? No, why? Do you feel ill? Or are you seeing things?"

"No, I just…" She let that sentence trail off. There was no way she could confess this foolishness to him, a complete stranger.

Finn wandered to her windows. For a long moment, he stood, hands folded behind his back, staring out toward the woods where the pool lay. Bree let him think in peace. Frankly, she needed a little time to get her own thoughts in order too.

Finally, with a sigh, he turned to face her. "Ms. Williams, would you like me to tell you the truth? About why I want that spring so badly?"

"Yes. Of course." The truth was always best.

"All right." He drew a deep breath and stood, feet planted wide like a marine at attention. "Have you ever heard of Shifters?"

"Shifters? Um, no."

"Grandma didn't tell you any stories? You've never Shifted?"

"Shifted what?"

He rubbed his eyes and groaned. "Damn, this is going to be awkward. Okay, let's try this another way. Do you believe in astrology… magic… UFOs… ghosts… anything like that?"

Bree shook her head. Her house might be full of ghosts but that didn't mean she had to believe in them. Or confess to belief, anyway.

"Of course not." A long, tired sigh escaped him. "Well, I guess I'm going to have to prove to you that magic exists. All right, would you step outside with me, please?"

Finn Donnelly was quickly slipping from 'intriguing' to 'crazy'. "Why can't you show me your 'magic' in here?"

"Because it's big magic. Magic larger than a bus. Won't fit well in your living room."

Well, at least he wasn't pulling a coin from behind her ear. Bree followed him out, keeping a safe distance between them. If he lost his marbles, she was bolting for Nielsen's house. Her neighbor might be a jerk, but he was a *safe* jerk.

The sun had dipped below the western hills of Jackson Hole. In the evening gloom, she couldn't read his face. "I'm probably going to make things worse by saying this," he grumbled, "but don't be scared."

"So, this is 'scary' magic?" She questioned, glad she had sensible shoes on. The odds of a sprint to Nielsen's seemed to be growing.

"Not to me, no. But the first time you see someone Shift, it can be startling."

"Okay. Sure. I'll try to stay calm during this… shifty magic." Finn Donnelly was now officially as creepy as her ghosts.

Her face must have given her away, because he gave a sour prediction: "This is going to end badly…"

Without warning, the air around him writhed. Curtains of energy, like heat waves on a summer highway, spilled across the lawn, twisting the universe itself. For a second, she lost sight of the man. He dissolved into white scales that exploded outward, filling the yard. Claws appeared, legs the size of trees and tipped with deadly talons. Wings unfurled overhead and suddenly, Finn Donnelly was gone.

A Dragon stood in front of her. Watching her with burning eyes like chips of glacial ice.

Her breath caught in her throat. Her eyes bulged, staring. At that maw that could swallow her in one bite. At those claws, tearing into the lawn. At the sheer, impossible *size* of this creature.

Without warning, the dam holding her emotions back collapsed, releasing a flood of terror and adrenaline.

And as panic washed over her, suddenly, she was falling, shrinking as she tumbled to the ground. Fur burst out across her body. She landed on all four, a tiny creature dwarfed by the patio chairs. Long ears twitched once, then plastered against her body.

Her last sane thought was, *Oh my God, I'm a rabbit!*

Then sanity shredded as another voice screamed in her head.

Predator! Predator! Predator! it wailed.

Bree stamped a warning and fled in terror.

Behind her, a roar exploded. "Bree! No, wait!"

The beat of wings, slowly and ponderous, sounded. Instinctively, she zigzagged, fearing that, at any second, the predator would pounce upon her.

Trees! Cover! Flee!

There! Across the road! Trees!

Bree abandoned her evasive maneuvers and simply bolted, skimming along the lawn like a furry bullet. Across the grass, leaping the ditch, onto the road and...

Like a star going nova, the world exploded into light. An all-consuming brilliance that devoured fear, destroyed thought. Helpless, frozen, Bree stared at it. Unable to do anything as the light swept toward her.

She heard a screech of car brakes... and the predator pounced.

But not on her.

CHAPTER 9

*O*kay, that had gone badly – even for one of his notoriously awful 'rescues'.

Slouched in an easy chair, Finn studied the woman he'd 'saved'. Bree was curled in a ball on the couch, shivering uncontrollably. Every now and then, her nose twitched violently. A sign that her Hare was rattled too.

"Would you like some whiskey?" he offered. "I find it helps in these types of situations."

"Th-th-these types?" Her teeth chattered. "Does this happen a lot with you?"

"Not a lot… technically. But I'm not a, uh, subtle guy. So, it happens often enough that I know whiskey takes the edge off."

She didn't answer.

Her shakes seemed weaker now. Probably a good sign. He considered just handing her the whiskey then decided that moving might not be wise.

"Nielsen," she croaked. "Is he all right?"

"The paramedics will check him out, but he should be fine."

"How can he be 'fine'?" she snapped. "A Dragon squashed his car!"

"Technically, I didn't 'squash' his car. I landed in front of him. He ran into *me.*"

This detail did not impress his Mate. "A *Dragon* landed in front of him! How is that not going to send him into therapy for years?"

"Because he's mortal. And the human brain refuses to see things it doesn't believe in." Her eyes narrowed in suspicion, but he shrugged. "Trust me. I have screwed up lots of times and Shifted in front of a normal person. They will hallucinate, faint, forget... you name it. Do pretty much *anything* except believe the 'impossible.' Last I heard, your neighbor was raving at the paramedics about his engine exploding. Swore he was going to sue Cadillac for selling him a defective car."

"Oh." Still queasy, she pondered his answer. Then her eyes lit with indignation. "Wait a second! I'm human too! Why could I see that thing?"

"That 'thing' was me. Saving *your* life. Hares are delicate. Getting hit by a car would kill one."

"Oh really?" The madder she got, the less she shivered. Finn guessed that was an improvement, even if it rankled to be called a 'thing.' "You wouldn't have had to 'save' me if you hadn't stampeded me into the road!"

That was too much! "I had *no* idea you were going to do something as hare-brained as... as... uh."

Bree's eyes narrowed. "Hare-brained? Seriously?"

"Sorry I, uh... heh." He scratched his nose, hoping to hide the way his lips curled into a smile.

Her lips were twitching too, though. "Hare-brained. Is this what I have to look forward to?"

"Hopefully not, no. With practice, you'll learn to control your Hare. In fact, why don't you try Shifting now?"

"Because I can *see* you. You have this… this energy. And sometimes, out of the corner of my eye, you look like a Dragon."

"Shifters recognize each other, yes. Why would that stop you from Shifting?"

Bree burst out in incredulous laughter. "The moment my rabbit spots you, it's going to fly straight into that plate glass door. I don't want to go splat like a bug on a windshield."

Huh. She had a point. Hares were pretty flighty.

"Nope. I've had enough excitement for one night."

"How about that whiskey then? I could use one myself."

As he promised, a couple shots of single malt calmed them both. Bree found a blanket. Wrapped in it, she listened quietly as he told her about the Shifter world. About his Flight and their enemies, the Fangs of Apophis. About the rebirth of the Wellsprings.

"So, the pool is one of these Wellsprings?"

"Yes." He poured himself another shot and offered to refill her glass, but she was still nursing her last one. "Gateways to the Other Side, the source of our Shifter souls."

"Gate, huh? So those things that are coming through – are they Shifter souls?"

Finn nearly dropped his drink. Even his Dragon snapped to attention. "There's something coming through your Wellspring? Into *this* world?"

"I think so." As so many women did, she grew flustered when the full force of his Dragon's attention fell on her. "I mean, I'm not sure."

Her hesitation vexed his Dragon and he felt his eyes burn with its annoyance.

Let me handle this, will you? Otherwise, we're going to be chasing a damned Hare all around this place.

It subsided, grumbling. "Tell me exactly what you saw," he urged Bree.

"There was a mist and figures in it. Tall, thin. More like pillars than people. Some were light, others shadowy."

Didn't sound like anything he'd ever heard of. "Are they still there?"

"I think they followed me home."

"They're here? Now?" Nothing appeared to him – but Hares were Witches by nature. Sensitives who saw things no other Shifter could see.

"Not now. They left when you came. That's why I was so nervous when you got here."

His Dragon gave a soft, protective growl. Finn agreed. Nothing good fled a Dragon.

Except, well, Hares. Watching the way Bree still clutched her blanket, he felt the touch of doubt. Maybe a Dragon would intimidate small spirits from the Other Side. Besides, Bree was his Mate. If these 'ghosts' meant her harm, he would have sensed it.

As he had at the restaurant.

"Did anything odd happen at lunch today?"

"I saw a shadow. A black puddle. It crept across the floor and then seemed to... to..." Her eyes locked on his and she trembled. "You won't believe me."

"I'm a Dragon. I don't have trouble believing strange things."

Her laughter, bright and relieved, made his heart skip a beat. "You don't know how good it feels to hear that. I thought I was going mad."

"So, what did this shadow do?"

"It seemed to possess Daven. His eyes went dead black and... well, he can be a jerk, but he'd never hurt me. Like he did."

"And it fled when I showed up?"

"Yes. By the way, how did you know something was wrong?"

And there it was. The ugly, sad elephant in the room. The one bit of Shifter lore he'd give his soul to avoid.

Should he call it a hunch? She'd believe him if he did. Maybe someday, years in the future, she'd learn about the Rite of Claiming. He'd be long gone by then, though, and this pathetic 'Mating' as well.

That was the coward's path. He had a lot of flaws, but a lack of nerve wasn't one of them.

Bree deserved the true.

And he deserved another shot before he did this.

One of her eyebrows rose as he gulped his whiskey down. "I'm guessing this is a touchy subject?"

"You could say that. Did you have a particularly vivid dream Friday night?"

"Yes! How did you... oh! Oh my!" With a squeak, she clapped a hand over her mouth. He poured himself another shot as, one by one, the pieces of the puzzle fell in place for her.

"So, we're Mates? All that stuff about eternal love and soul mates... that's true?"

"No. And yes. I did Claim you. That means I can sense when you're in danger."

"That's why you came running back?"

"Yes. That shadow – unlike these 'ghosts' in your house – meant you harm."

"So, we're, like, married or something." She twisted the ring on her left hand.

Her *engagement* ring.

"No." Ignoring his Dragon's mournful keen, he leaned forward. "I meant what I said, I don't believe in Fate. We have free will, no matter what people tell us."

Bile rose in his throat, a reflection of the fire burning in his agitated Dragon. Finn swallowed, forcing it down. *He* was in charge, not the great serpent.

She kept fiddling with that ring. The expensive, gaudy proof of their problem. "Why did that happen?"

"That's my Dragon's way of telling me it likes you." Not exactly true. In fact, his Dragon seethed with fury at his flippant words. The Rite of Claiming revealed the other half of a Dragon's soul – not a hot babe he might get along with. Yet, his light tone seemed to put Bree at ease. And that was worth upsetting his Dragon.

"Wild sex means 'I like you'?"

"Yeah." They both laughed, even though he could feel the anger of his stewing soul.

"So, we don't have to… I don't know. Be an item?"

"No. Not if we don't want to." With all his heart, he prayed he was right.

He might not be – if there was any truth in the old stories. A Mate was half of a true Dragon's soul. What man could live with only half a soul?

He didn't know. Maybe he'd find out.

Round and round went that ring. "I like you. I think," she added. "Not that I know you much, but… You know I'm engaged, right? So, I can't…"

"I know. I'm not looking for a Mate either. So, we're in agreement."

Or, rather, two of them were in agreement. His Dragon still longed to challenge Daven and drive that unworthy male from his Mate's life.

"Okay, good." Was she relieved – or sad? Damned if he could tell. Women were hard to read. "Hang on! If that dream was real, why did my stupid rabbit flip out when it saw your Dragon? Wouldn't it remember you?"

"Ask it."

Bree's nose wrinkled. "I don't want to talk to a Hare," she whispered. "It feels… oh!" A flash of shock crossed her face. "It's… stomping. Stomping *inside* of me!"

He chuckled. "Get used to that. You've annoyed your Shifter soul – and it's going to let you know. From now on, internal debates will be a regular thing. I argue with my Dragon all the time."

"As for your question," he shrugged. "You probably startled it. *You* were frightened, and your Hare got overwhelmed by that."

"So, it really is Hare-brained," she groaned. "Arrgh. There it goes, thumping all around."

The whiskey had done its job, melting pain and grief into a gentle melancholy. Reminding him that yes, his life was still a mess. But when wasn't it? He'd get through this, just like he'd gotten through everything else.

Bree pushed her shot glass away. "Well, you've successfully flipped my life upside down. What now?"

"Two things. First, I need to call my Flight. Your 'ghosts' have given me an idea."

"Sure. And then?"

"Then we pay a visit to the pool." She paled. The urge to pull her into his arms, to protect her, swept over him. "I will make sure nothing happens to you. Remember, I can sense when you're in danger. The minute there's any risk, I'll get you out."

"Okay." There was a distinct lack of enthusiasm in her tone. Not that he could blame her. She didn't really know him, or how protective Dragons truly were. He'd die before he'd lead her into danger.

"Let's start with the easy part. I assume you've got Skype or something like it on your computer?"

She did. While she got it set up, he called Brandon Lorde and filled his Alpha in on the developments. "You said Tess Morland was at your Wellspring, yes? Could you get her in front of the computer?"

Lorde frowned. "Is it important?"

"Very."

"All right then. I'll wake her."

Eh, right. He'd forgotten they were on the East Coast. It was past midnight there.

Bree waved him toward the computer, but he shook his head. "You need to do this. There's a woman I want you to look at. She's a Shifter, an odd one. I want to know what her soul looks like to you."

Several minutes later, a disheveled woman wearing nothing more than a man's t-shirt staggered in front of the screen, yawning. Bed-head only improved her beauty. She looked like a Hollywood diva, unjustly awoken, not a new mother who'd been dragged out of bed in the middle of the night.

"My, my," he chuckled. "Asleep before midnight? How far the Bad Girl has fallen!"

Tess flipped him the bird mid-yawn. "Screw you, Finn. Wait till you have a baby that won't sleep through the night. You'll be passing out at noon."

Beside him, Bree tensed. Her head twisted from side to side as she stared at the screen sideways.

"You gonna introduce me to your Hare friend?"

"Oh, right. This is Bree Williams. One of the Lost, like you used to be. Tonight, she learned she's a Witch Hare."

"Ha! That brings back memories!" An impish grin lit the other woman's face. "Nothing like having your life explode, is there?"

"Bree, this is Tess Morland. She's the Mate of one of my Flight. And she's a very unusual type of Shifter."

She squinted at the screen and nibbled on her lip. "I can't see her Bunny or Dragon or whatever she's supposed to have."

"Most Shifters can't. Do you see anything, though?"

"Yeah. She's haunted. There's a white shadow hovering around her."

"Yes!" Finn crowed in triumph. "I thought so. Lorde! We have Adanai at this Wellspring. They're active. They're venturing out into the countryside. And at least one of them was hostile."

All traces of fatigue vanished from Tess' face and his Alpha leaned down. "This could be a breakthrough. I'll gather some Hares, summon the Flight, and we'll be there tomorrow morning. Tess? We'll need you too."

"Right. I'll tell Darian he's on baby duty. See you in a bit, Finn. Hey, Bree? Sorry, babe, but the dial on your Crazy-Meter is going to get turned to eleven."

That was what he loved about his Flight. No hesitation, no delay. They had your back. "I'm going to go check on the Wellspring itself. Bree says it changed two days ago."

"Don't. Our intelligence," Lorde glanced at Tess as she trotted off, "suggests the Adanai have weapons capable of harming Dragons. Wait for backup."

The delay chafed – but it also meant he wouldn't need to take Bree out there. That pacified his Dragon.

Once contact information was exchanged, he ended the conference.

Arms wrapped around herself, his Mate sat, a small, frightened bundle of nerves.

Hell, he hadn't even thought about her. How mad must this all seem? Her first Shift, a brush with becoming road kill, and now a horde of witches and Dragons were going to descend on her home.

All in one night.

He laid a hand on her shoulder. Tiny tremors, too light for him to see, shook her. "You all right?"

The smile she turned on him was too bright to be believable. "Sure. What's an Ada... Adan...?"

"Adanai. Think of them as faeries. Almost all of them stayed on the Other Side."

"That other world. Where your… where *our* Shifter souls come from?"

He caught that correction. Good. She was beginning to accept the impossible. "That's right. Tess is the only one we know of who Shifted to this world along with our Kinds."

"And now, a bunch of Hares and Dragons and Tess are coming here? To look at my pool?"

He nodded. Bree rocked back and forth, then nodded too. "I guess that's okay."

Ah, hell. Permission. He should have asked for that *first,* before filling her home with lunatics. "Sorry about that."

"But we don't have to go out there tonight?"

"No." The relief in her face made him long to pull her into his arms and reassure her that this would all work out, somehow. That he'd keep her safe, no matter how crazy things got. "I'm going back to town. Will you be all right by yourself?"

"No. I can't stay here alone."

Her refusal caught him flat-footed. "I could…"

Could what?

Offer to stay here with her? Could he do that? Sleep on the couch like a friend, not a Mate? Abandon her in her bed, frightened and lonely? No, that was a recipe for disaster. He'd never hold himself back. Something would happen. He'd try to comfort her. And… he'd made a mess of everything.

Like usual.

Either she'd resent his advance – or she'd accept it, and he'd break up her engagement. Something she didn't deserve.

"I could…"

But Bree wasn't waiting to hear what he 'could' do. She was already heading for the stairs to her room. "I'm going to stay in a hotel tonight. Would you wait while I grab some things? You keep those ghosts at bay."

"Sure," he said, fighting to keep the disappointment from his voice.

It was the least he could do.

And probably the best thing he could do too.

CHAPTER 10

The next day, Bree stayed *well* away from her house. Tucked in a nice Jacuzzi suite at the Prana Wellness Resort, she ate room service and waited for news.

Calls arrived steadily throughout the day. First, it was her private eye, Jenna Magnuson, promising to drop off the completed dossier on Finn Donnelly.

Next, Daven invited her to lunch. She blew him off, claiming she wanted a spa day. Pressure from the Luxe deal... time to think about the wedding... Prana Wellness would settle her frayed nerves. When she hung up, she was glumly surprised at how easy it was to lie to him. And how little that bothered her.

Throughout the morning, Finn rang several times, diligently keeping her in the loop. His Flight had arrived. Six Witch Hares were here. Preliminary examination confirmed that the pool was an active Wellspring, one that showed surprising levels of power (whatever that meant). Then silence – until late in the afternoon when the phone rang once more.

"Don't go home," he told her. "It's not safe."

"Why? What happened?"

"Tess tried to speak to the Adanai and they turned violent."

Bree's mouth went dry. "Oh my god, is she okay?" She hadn't known the woman long, but she'd seemed nice – and she was a new mother too!

"Not really." Finn's voice was a grim murmur. "She'll live, but we're at the hospital now. For Tess, and because one of my Flight took an arrow to the chest. Sliced right through his scales. Didn't think that was possible. Guess I should have believed Tess' stories."

"Are *you* okay?" That question terrified her more than she wanted to admit.

"I'm fine." Disgust filled his voice, like that was a shameful thing to admit. "I was in the back. Covered their retreat. But it was my Alpha who got Tess out."

"Well, you said you're injured, right?"

"Yeah."

Phones were a miserable way to deliver bad news. If only he was here, where she could hold him, wrap the big man in her arms and...

...do all kinds of things that were *not* appropriate for someone engaged to be married.

She could go down to the hospital...

And do what? You don't know any of these people except Finn. You're a novice, virtually a child, in their world. You'd be underfoot all the time. A pest.

But he'd be there. And she could...

No. Maybe she had serious second thoughts about this marriage. Until she actually gave up on it, though, her relationship with Finn *had* to stay just friendly.

So, she didn't offer to come down – and he didn't invite

her. A fact that threw a pall over an already gloomy day. It would have been nice to be wanted, even if she shouldn't go. A petty, selfish thought. Yet, one she couldn't deny.

The last phone call came from the front desk. They had a package for her from Jenna Magnuson. The dossier on Finn Donnelly. Bree scrambled to get it.

It was research. Just research. Nothing wrong with that, right?

At first glance, Jenna's thin folder disappointed. Worse, the cover letter was an apology:

Ms. Williams:

Initial inquiries didn't turn up much. I got financials and real estate holdings but surprisingly little personal information. I can expand my investigations if you're interested. I did locate articles on his family. It appears that 'Finn' is a traditional name for these Donnellys. Not sure this information is useful, but it's enclosed.

Let me know how you want to pursue this.

Jenna

Finn had a... family?

Well, why shouldn't he? she asked herself – even as her stomach sank. He'd never said anything about his personal life. No reason she should think he was single.

Available. Be honest. That's what you really wanted.

Served her right for jumping to conclusions.

Flipping quickly, she skimmed the report. Finn was rich. Of course. The very idea of an impoverished Dragon was ludicrous. No college. No club memberships. No social media accounts. Yet, no marriages or births either.

Odd. Where was this 'family'?

A quarter of the way through the slender folder, she found them. Or rather, 'him.'

Jenna had built a proposed family tree for Finn. One she found odd.

FINN DONNELLY. NO BIRTH DATE, NO MARRIAGE. SON OF...
Finn Donnelly and Lena Carlisle. Son of...
Finn Donnelly and Grace Adams. Son of...
Finn Donnelly and Sara Noleski. Son of...

ON AND ON THE LIST WENT. THE WOMEN DIED, USUALLY young. Four were killed in accidents. Two disappeared. Tuberculosis claimed one, cancer two.

The 'men'? No deaths or personal information on any of them. A fact that baffled Jenna, but to Bree, the solution was obvious.

They were all one man. Her Finn. Dragons were either immortal or damn close to it.

These are his *wives. They're the women he's loved.*

The women he *lost*. Not one had lived to forty.

The world seemed to tilt beneath her as she studied the clippings. She was a Hare. Did this mean that she, too, would live forever?

How could she marry Daven, knowing that he would grow old and die in the course of a normal lifetime?

Not that any of Finn's wives made it that long. Fires, car accidents, hit and runs... one by one, they died, 'taken too early.'

Just like her parents, who drowned on vacation and left her to be raised by her grandmother. A tragic accident... or so she'd been told.

Looking at that list of Finn's losses, her faith in bad luck withered. No one was this cursed. This was the work of an enemy – probably the Fangs of Apophis that he'd mentioned.

And if the Fangs murdered these women, why not her parents? They had to have been Shifters too.

Bree flopped back against the soft, cotton pillows and stared numbly at the ceiling. Everything she thought she knew – about the world, her life, her past – was falling apart.

No wonder Finn said he didn't know if he could go through this again.

Hell, she wasn't sure she could go through a marriage even once – let alone ten times.

Time passed. The television muttered in the background while she ignored it, her mind tossed by warring emotions. Anger, shock, pity for Finn and her parents. Too many thoughts, too many feelings to make sense.

Eventually, her grumbling stomach reminded her that living things needed to eat. She ordered a hamburger and a bottle of wine then curled back up until room service's knock drew her out of her funk.

When she opened the door, Daven – not dinner – waited for her.

"Hey, babe!" A peck on the cheek and he breezed past her. "Damn, you look terrible. Are you okay?"

"Yeah. I was lying down." Close enough to the truth.

Today, she couldn't look at her fiancé in the same inno-cent way. He was human – while she was a Shifter. What did that mean for them? Twenty years from now, he'd have grey hair. His youthful vigor would crumble as he slid into old age. And her? She wouldn't look a day older.

Could she still love him? She *thought* so – but could anyone know for sure?

One thing she did know, however, is that Daven would hate her. As she watched him, he paused in front of the mirror and whisked a stray hair back into place. He was proud of his looks. He'd die of jealousy if they faded while hers remained.

"Why don't you get cleaned up and we can catch dinner?"

"I'd love to, but I already ordered room service."

"So, cancel it. It's only money."

Now what? Having said 'I'd love to' made it awkward to admit that, honestly, tonight, she just wanted to hide from the world. Once more, like always, Bree found herself going with the flow just to avoid a scene.

"Sure! Give me a minute to freshen up."

So much for the great 'predator.' Maybe she really was a bunny.

A 'thump' from deep inside her warned that her Hare didn't appreciate being dissed like that.

New dress. Fresh makeup. Teeth and hair brushed. Ten minutes later, when she stepped out of the bathroom, she almost felt good about getting outside.

"Ready?"

Daven sat on her bed, the pages of the 'Finn Donnelly' report strewn around him. He didn't look up when she spoke.

"You're really obsessed with this guy, aren't you?"

Oh, for crying out loud, not this again! "No, I'm not. I asked Jenna to look into him."

"Do you investigate everyone who looks at property near you?"

"Yes. All the ones that offer me four times my asking price, anyway."

"Four times?" Greed startled him out of his sulk.

"Yup. Now you understand my 'sudden' interest in selling." Not true – but he'd never believe that faerie ghosts made her house intolerable. Hell, even she barely believed it!

"I hope you've accepted! That's a fortune!"

"Not yet. I just got the report a couple hours ago."

"Why did you want all this crap?"

"Because what if four times isn't enough?" Lies spilled out, a spider's web of untruth that sounded oh so plausible. "What if he's in mining – and knows there's gold under this area? Or he works for some state legislator and has insider knowledge of a project that will raise property values?"

"That's my shark!" Daven murmured lovingly, as if that was the sexiest thing you could say to a woman. He tossed the financials back on the bed and came to her, wrapping his arms around her waist. "So, does he know something?"

"Not that I can see, no. Just seems to be a rich eccentric who's in love with the artesian spring on my land."

"Mmm." He nuzzled her neck, slipping the strap of her dress down her shoulder.

Dammit, if he kept this up, she'd have to get dressed *again*.

The thought filled her with shame. Seriously, her fiancé came onto her and the only thing she cared about was her dress? That was not a good sign.

A nudge, and the other strap slipped off. Freed, the whole dress started to slide down. "How about we skip dinner and do something more interesting? Ever made love in a Jacuzzi?"

She had – with him, in fact. Twice. Guess that hadn't been as memorable to him as it was to her.

Whiskers flaring, ears alert, her Hare came alive. Bree could feel it stirring inside her. Sensing some current of Fate she couldn't see.

So that was the source of her intuition? Those uncanny hunches and lucky guesses that sent her career skyrocketing? Fate flowed like a river around living creatures. And her soul, her Hare, could sense its movements.

Now it warned her that she stood on the brink of a precipice. What she chose now would change her world.

How, Bree had no idea. But this was the fulcrum, the crisis. Her answer to this question would set her Fate.

What question? she asked her Hare. *Whether or not to have sex in a hot tub?* That's *the question that determines my Fate for all time?*

Thumper stayed silent, its ears swiveling madly.

Her silken dress slithered down around her ankles, leaving her standing in just her underwear. Daven, not waiting for her answer, cupped her breasts.

I need to decide soon, or this decision is going to get made for me.

Did she want to make love to Daven? Not right now, no. She was tired, hungry, and upset. But it wouldn't be the first time she'd gotten talked into a fling. Daven was hot and, clearly, ready to go right now. With a little effort, she could get into the mood herself. No big deal. Why not?

Thump.

Her Hare approved of that question.

Okay, why not? Well, she was tired. All she really wanted to do was eat and go to bed.

Thump thump thump thump thump.

Wrong answer, that flurry of stamps said.

All she really wanted was…

…to have Finn show up, uninvited and unexpected. He'd take her in his arms, promise that everything would be all right. That she had a place in this mad new world. That he would protect her from the monsters out there.

Bree stiffened as the problem came into focus.

What she *really* wanted was another man.

Not her fiancé.

Having done its job, her Hare huddled up in a small ball and waited for her decision.

If she had any doubts, she needed to postpone the wedding. Yet, some instinct warned her that Daven wouldn't tolerate being put on hold. Ready or not, the decision was here.

Did she love Daven? No, not really. On Friday, that didn't bother her. When he proposed, she didn't believe love existed. Now...

Now, she wondered.

About the way the world lit up every time she saw Finn. The safety she felt when he was near. His solid, unshakable honesty. The flutters that filled her stomach when they touched. The aching grief that filled her when she read about the women he'd lost.

Was that love?

She didn't know. But whatever it was, it was beautiful. A rainbow running from passion to grief, holding every emotion she could name. It filled her life with wonder and joy. Under its light, the future became a glorious adventure – not a tedious slog toward death.

With Daven, none of that existed.

'Love' or not, didn't that answer the question?

"Daven, stop." Gently, she pushed his hands away. "Not right now. I'm tired and really hungry."

"I could get some fruit. Feed you in the hot tub." He reached for her again.

"Sorry, not tonight." Backing away, she headed for the closet with its complementary bath robe. Easier than trying to snatch up her dress from between his feet.

THUMP THUMP THUMP!

One quick warning, then her Hare vanished.

What was wrong with that creature? Sure, Daven was upset. Once more, that annoying pout spoiled his good looks. Arms folded tight across his chest telegraphed his displeasure. He was angry.

But dangerous? No. This was Daven, after all. The man was not dangerous.

Was he?

Then why had her Hare bolted down some mystical rabbit hole?

"It's because of that asshole, isn't it?"

"Daven, stop. I'm just tired." Her Hare might think this was a one-way street, but Bree wanted to keep her options open if she could.

"I saw you two holding hands," he spat.

"For the last time, we *weren't* holding hands!"

"I *saw* you!" he wailed, his voice rising to a shrill cry. "Not a week after we got engaged and you were already hitting on some other guy!"

"The hell I was!" she screamed back. Let the people in the next room hear. She didn't give a damn.

Daven laughed and closed his eyes. "I am *such* an idiot!"

A cool draft whispered through the room, raising goosebumps along her bare arms. Daven stilled, his words growing softer. "And he doesn't even realize that, by that point, you had already given yourself to another."

Who didn't realize what? That accusation didn't make a bit of sense.

Until her fiancé opened his eyes and there was nothing there except darkness. "Your vows wither before the moon grows full again. And yet, you babble of devotion that will last eternity."

Suddenly, her Hare's flight made perfect sense. Without a word, Bree made like a rabbit and dashed into the bathroom, slamming the door behind her.

Click. The lock snapped shut.

Soft footsteps approached. Muttered words, like a pool of filth, spilled under the door. "...faithless... fickle... polluted...muddled..."

The knob rattled. Bree backed away, searching for a

weapon. Toilet paper? Jeez, no. The shower rod? Flimsy as hell.

BANG! The creature threw itself against the door.

Aha! The toilet! She snatched the lid off the tank. Hefty and solid, her makeshift 'bat' took the edge off her fear.

BANG! With a crack, the frame began to splinter.

A dull 'thud' echoed from outside. A tremor ran through the floor and suddenly, the night air along with the shrieks of car alarms filled the room.

Finn! That had to be the sound of a Dragon landing in a parking lot. A wild, delirious grin spread across her face.

My Mate. He knows I'm in danger.

BANG! The crack widened, and her relief shriveled. Finn might be here. But he was outside – and he wouldn't make it in time.

The lid in her hands was a cold, deadly weight. Could she really bash someone with it? No, not 'someone'. *Daven.* Her former fiancé. He might not be in control of himself, but it was his body she'd have to hurt.

Or even kill.

Unless she could think of a better plan.

Like… do what she did best. Talk!

Ignoring her Hare's urge to run, Bree forced herself to inch closer to the door. "Hey, hello? Guy on the other side? What's your name?"

A hiss of disgust, as if a cockroach had crept up and addressed him. "Names have power. I will not give you mine."

"Fair enough. You can talk about your grievances, though, can't you?"

"Grievances."

Okay, not very chatty. But at least he'd stopped throwing Daven's body at the door. "Maybe if I understand your position better, we can find common ground. Right now, I don't understand your goals."

"You should be shredded."

'Shredded.' Creepy as hell. Though that was the second time he'd used that freaky word. "Why do I need to be shredded?"

"To separate."

Come *on*, Finn! "Separate what, precisely?"

"The pure and impure."

"What's impure in me?" If you wanted people to run on at the mouth, ask for complaints, not compliments.

Sure enough, the shadow thing began to rave, snarling about pollution and unclean mixing of 'adan' and 'oru.' Who knew what those things were?

Bree didn't, and didn't care. As long as he kept raving, it didn't matter what he babbled about. All she needed to do was wind him up. A prod here, a prompt there. A few questions to keep him ranting until...

With a tremendous crash, the door to her room shattered.

Sorry, Mr. Monster. My Dragon's not bouncing off a door three times.

"What the hell are you doing?" Finn roared.

A loud, unmanly yelp suggested Daven was in control of his body once again.

"Finn, wait!" Hoping to save the poor lawyer from unnecessary pain, Bree yanked the door open.

The Dragon stood, feet planted wide, one hand closed around the front of Daven's shirt. The lawyer back-peddled furiously, feet slipping on the rug. Finn held him with effortless ease and when he spotted her, nearly naked, an eerie flame lit his blue eyes.

"Did this worm hurt you?" he snarled through gritted teeth.

"No! Adanai!"

That word cut through the Dragon's growing rage. "Still here?"

She shook her head.

"Let go of me, you asshole!"

Finn did. Threat gone, he spared the other man no more thought than a gnat. "Are you all right, Bree?"

'Bree.' Not 'Ms. Williams.' And even though he tried to hide it, she saw how his hand rose, instinctively, toward her. How his first urge was to comfort her.

"Yes. I'm fine. Just startled. And," her nose wrinkled as she remembered what she was (not) wearing, "half naked."

Released from the Dragon's grasp, Daven recovered his courage. "You're in big trouble, buddy. That was assault! I don't give a damn who you are! I'm calling the police."

Eyes narrowing, Finn turned toward the lawyer like a mastiff rounding on an irate Chihuahua.

Time to break this up for good. "No, Daven, you're not calling the police. If you do, you'll have to explain why you chased me into the bathroom and almost broke down the door. All because I didn't want to go to bed with you."

That was a low blow, since it hadn't really been 'him' who assaulted her. But she was tired, and hungry, and sick of Daven's posturing.

As she'd hoped, that threat doused his anger immediately. "Bree, I… I don't know what came over me. I'm sorry."

"I know. But you need to leave, now."

Daven edged toward the door. Finn watched him, tense – a sight that infuriated the lawyer once more. "He needs to leave too."

"That's for *me* to decide, not you." She finally found the hotel bathrobe and wrapped it around herself.

"Dammit, Bree, you are *my* fiancée! Mine!"

Her Hare had been right. A melancholy relief welled up within her. Everything changed the moment she turned

Daven down. All that remained was to say the words. To acknowledge the choice she'd already made.

"Daven, I don't think we'd make a good couple. I'm calling the wedding off."

"Bree, you can't be serious..." He seemed genuinely surprised. As if he had no idea why kicking in a bathroom door would give a woman second thoughts about marriage.

"I'm sorry. I was drunk. I shouldn't have ever have said yes."

"I can't believe you're dumping me for some gorilla."

"I'm not choosing someone over you." Was that true? Honestly, she didn't know. "I just don't think we should get married."

"Why?"

Silently, she pointed at the splintered bathroom door. "Among other things."

Daven had the grace to blush. "Fine. If you're dumping me, give my ring back. You don't get to keep that."

"Of course."

Bree tugged on the ring, but it wouldn't slide off her finger. "Hang on. It's stuck."

"Oh, sure," Daven sneered.

What on Earth was wrong with this thing? It turned on her finger easily, yet it would *not* fit over her knuckle.

...thump...

A soft, nervous warning from her Hare. Something was wrong.

"Look, I'm going to have to see a jeweler to get this off."

"If you damage it, you're paying for it! I can still get my money back."

So much for true love, eh? "Don't worry. I'll be careful."

"Or you could try losing some weight." Funny how much meaner he got when things didn't go his way.

That jibe pushed Finn over the edge. "You need to leave. Now."

One last venomous glare and Daven retreated out the door. "You're going to regret this, Bree Williams! You're finished in this town!"

The Dragon took a step forward – which sent Daven fleeing down the hall.

CHAPTER 11

When the door closed, Finn's shoulders slumped. "Oh, hell, Bree. I am so sorry."

"Why?" She slipped an arm around his broad shoulders. "I am so happy you're here."

"I just destroyed your engagement."

"You saved me a lot of pain and embarrassment. Maybe even my life."

"From that bum? Please." Still caught up in the anger of the confrontation, he didn't melt into her embrace as she'd hoped. He simply endured it.

"It's the bums of the world you have to worry about. Strong men don't pick on the weak. I bet *you*," she gave his imposing bicep a squeeze, "have never chased a woman into a bathroom."

"Not unless she wanted me to, no." Slowly, the tension drained away as his body realized it wouldn't face a fight.

So, what now? The room was wrecked. The damage to the bathroom door wasn't too bad but Finn had snapped a hinge when he plowed in.

"Guess I need to go downstairs and apologize to the management."

"Let me do that," he protested. "Pack your things. I'll get you another room."

Here? Where Daven expected to find her? She'd never be able to sleep, even with three locks on the door. And would any place else be better – or could that thing infesting Daven's body track her down?

No, there was only one thing that seemed to keep these 'Adanai' at bay. And she wasn't leaving his side.

"Finn, can I ask you a favor?"

"Anything. If it's in my power, it's yours." Eyes like blue lasers fixed upon her. Damn, he was an intense man!

Intensely *good*. She trusted him, with a faith no other man had ever won from her. Honest, loyal, devoted, strong... They'd only known each other for a few days, and already, she could sing his praises for hours. Deep inside her, an unfamiliar feeling stirred. Joy and desire woven together. An unshakeable confidence that, as long as he was here, every-thing would be all right. By his side, she felt safe, no matter what dangers loomed. There was no place she'd rather be.

Was that... love? It felt so different from the shallow desires that Daven roused in her.

"Could I stay with you tonight? I know what you must be thinking!" A blush crept onto her cheeks. "'Wow, that's the fastest rebound sex ever.' And that's not what I mean at all."

"Actually, what I thought was that you must be fright-ened." There was no disdain in his voice, just acceptance. "No assumptions, either. You're welcome to the bed. The couch will suit me just fine."

"Thank you. I can't tell you how much that means right now."

She reached for him, but he turned from her. Her fingers brushed his arm, and then he was gone, out of reach. "Let's get you packed, shall we? I'll pay for the damage on the way out."

"Sure." Quickly, she retrieved her makeup from the bathroom. When she returned, she found him studying the papers scattered across the bed.

"So, I guess you've found out about me." The frost etched into his words chilled her.

"Finn, I'm sorry. I didn't mean to pry."

"You have a right to know what kind of a man Claimed you." Forgiving words – but he refused to look at her as he said them.

Shame welled up, and guilt for the pain she'd brought him. "I wanted to know who was trying to buy my spring."

No response. Finn collected the papers and slipped them back into their folder. Though, at least he didn't storm out or retreat when she inched closer. "Can you forgive me?"

"There's nothing to forgive."

"But you're angry with me." This time, he didn't shy away when she laid a hand on his arm.

"Embarrassed, not angry. You sure you want to entrust yourself to such a miserable 'protector'?"

"You're not miserable. No one can watch another person 24-7!"

He scooped up her suitcase, breaking the contact between them. "You need to, if you want to keep people safe."

"Or those people accept the risk. From what you told me about the Fangs of Apophis, I'm guessing life isn't particularly safe around a Dragon."

"It's not." His voice dropped to a low, gravelly murmur. "Especially for people who don't have a Dragon's thick scales."

Bree gathered her few belongings and tucked them into the day-bag. Every instinct urged her to drop the subject. Yet, there was one secret she could never endure. One detail from those pages of death and suffering that would drive her mad.

"Finn... two of those women disappeared. I know that was years ago, but are you still looking for them? Is there still hope?"

Not 'hope' for her: fear. If there was another woman out there, someone he still loved and desperately sought, she needed to know that.

To her relief and shame, he shook his head. "I know where they're buried."

"Oh. They were killed." What a miserable thing to be relieved about! How selfish could she be?

"I killed them."

Her heart skipped a beat at that. Finn met her gaze with his usual grim, steady calm. "Twice now, one of the Fangs has masqueraded as an eligible young lady. I guess I'm not a very good judge of character."

"And you had to... to..."

"Yes. One tried to shoot me. One planted a car bomb in my Jeep. Both of them spied on my Flight for years, thanks to me."

To be betrayed by your love... to realize that all their affection, their 'devotion' was nothing but a ruse... How could a man dare to love again after that?

Finn, however, misread her hesitation. "Does that make you hate me?"

"No, of course not! I admire you. After all this pain, you were still willing to Claim me."

With a snort, he grabbed her bag and headed for the door. "Then you must be as big a fool as I am."

CHAPTER 12

Three hours, two hamburgers and one blank check for 'hotel damages' later, Bree was starting to feel human again. A long soak in a hot bath settled her rattled nerves. As did the bottle of chardonnay that Finn dug up. Now, wrapped in an oversized, fluffy bathrobe, she watched the Dragon unfold a hide-a-bed couch.

"Skyline Resort has a nice view of the Tetons. Not that that's much use at night," he admitted.

Personally, that wasn't the view she was admiring. What caught her eye was the ease and grace with which he moved, so unusual in a big man. The bulge of his muscles and the way they made any task simple. The craggy lines of his face, weathered by pain and battle.

He was gorgeous. Not with the delicate beauty of a model. No, Finn's allure was something rougher. Tougher, more masculine. The beauty of a perfectly trained, hardened body. One powerful enough to face – and defeat – any enemy.

At work, Bree often dreamed of being a predator. A wolf, fleecing the sheep of the world.

How silly those thoughts seemed. Finn was the real deal. A soldier. A warrior. And yes, a killer. None of that frightened her, now that she understood why the world needed men like him.

To protect others from the monsters that lurked in the shadows.

"Hey." She leaned against the door frame, making no effort to hide how much she enjoyed watching him. "You don't have to sleep out here."

"I don't think it's wise for us to be together." Despite his words, she noticed he couldn't tear his eyes away from her long, bare legs.

Bree let her robe slide open a bit more. The couch cushion, forgotten, slipped from his hands. "Why not? Look, I won't make you swear that you'll never leave me or that we'll be real Mates after tonight. I know you can't give me that kind of promise."

He shook his head, regret darkening his blue eyes. Yet, even as he denied his longing, he drifted toward her. As if her love was a flame he couldn't resist.

Maybe in the morning she'd feel bad about seducing him. Now, she didn't care. Hunger and loneliness burned too bright within her. The cord that closed her robe parted and she let it slide to the floor. Revealing her tall, lithe body in all its golden splendor.

"Stay with me tonight. Please."

"Bree…" Closer he came, still denying the inevitable.

"I don't know what we'll want in the morning. But tonight, I want you."

Like a dam cracking under the force of pent up waters, his reserve shattered. Finn was at her side in two swift strides. As in her dream, strong arms closed around her, sweeping her off her feet.

Once he had promised her that life could be as sweet as that dream. She intended to make him prove that.

Cradled in his arms, Bree savored the delicious surrender, trusting in his strength. With ease, he carried her to the bed and set her down. Towering above her, he popped open the buttons of his shirt one by one, revealing broad pecs and curly hair.

Eagerly, she reached for his pants. The rounded bulge of his manhood, already roused, pressed against her fingertips. Four buttons, and it too was freed as he slid the jeans down the steel cordons of his thighs.

Masculine, nearly naked, he stood above her. Bree kissed the flat, sculpted plane of his stomach and felt him stiffen with pleasure at her touch. Her lips rose, exploring his abs, the curve of his ribs. Weaving her arms around him, she rose, feeling the cotton of his briefs rasp across her bare skin. Beneath it, the hot, demanding power of his sex awaiting its release.

Growing eager, he pulled her to her feet. Their lips joined in a long, slow kiss, and his hands began their own exploration. Stroking her hair, gliding down her back, circling the mounds of her buttocks. Still that scrap of cotton mocked her, rubbing against the slit of her legs as she pressed herself to him.

His lips broke free from hers, leaving a delicious ache at their loss. Kisses – yearning, eager – brushed down her throat, down her shoulders. Panting, she offered her breasts to his hungry mouth.

He nuzzled them softly, almost reverently. Lips traced her aureoles, circling her nipples. His tongue lashed across them and the nubs of her breasts stiffened, drawing a gasp of pleasure from her. Sucking, teasing, he played with her, fanning her desire. With one arm, he held her as she leaned back. The other hand remained curled about her buttocks. Stroking them, petting them. Stealing brushes against the curls between her legs. At each touch, she grew more damp, more eager for consummation.

Nipples hard, she whimpered as he played with her breasts. Then his mouth was falling, gliding down her silken stomach, lower and lower. Bree's breath caught as she realized what he sought.

Then his mouth found the dampness of her sex and she moaned out loud as his tongue slid across her clit. It lashed across her sex, driving her wild with every stroke. Her hips writhed, helpless, as she pressed herself against his hungry, devouring mouth.

Passion swelled, threatening to overwhelm her. "Wait!" she gasped. "Wait! I can't…"

Those delicious caresses paused. Bree shivered, shaking with a longing, a need fiercer than any she'd felt.

She should do something for him. She was selfish, too entangled in her own pleasure…

But as she silently berated herself, Finn finally slipped his briefs off. Freed from its cotton prison, his cock jutted forth. Hard, eager, demanding. Stoked by her cries, her pleasure, it was swollen with desire.

Ice blue eyes lit by Dragon's fire gazed up at her in love and longing. Then he wrapped his arms around her thighs and picked her up once more. Her heart raced – surely, he would throw her to the bed, now, and take her?

But the bed was not his goal. One step, and she felt the cool surface of the wall press against her back. He guided her legs around his waist. Bree clutched him tight, loving how his hard stomach pressed between her legs, teasing her sex once more. With a helpless whimper, she ground against him, seeking release from the maddening passion.

Then he lowered her gently… and she felt his long,

engorged cock slide into her. With a moan, her legs tightened, drawing him in fully.

Held aloft, caught in his arms, she felt a wild, primal passion sweep over her. Helpless, she gave herself to that animal desire. As he began to take her with hard, firm thrusts, she wrapped her legs tighter. Her body bucked, riding him even as he held her aloft.

Now, his own breath quickened. His proud mastery wavered as passion consumed him. Faster, harder, he drove, until his moans joined hers in a song of ecstasy. Waves of pleasure swept over her, washing away thought and care until nothing remained except the white pleasure that raged between her legs.

With a cry, he came. Her legs drew him tight one last time.

Once more, he raised her, separating them. Gently, he laid her down upon the sheets and, strength at last spent, he collapsed beside her.

No words were spoken. Their sweat-drenched bodies, their ragged breaths, bore witness to their pleasure.

Cuddled against him, still damp with the joy of their union, Bree smiled. Finn had told her the truth: with the right man, life could be as glorious as any dream.

CHAPTER 13

Mornings were magical. Slowly, rising out of the shreds of dreams, into consciousness. Feeling the warmth of his love beside him, curled against him. His body stirring at her touch, longing for Kirsten to turn to him and…

Kirsten?

That name jerked Finn awake, shattering the new day's innocent bliss.

Kirsten was dead. Drowned in the Missoula River. Investigators had been baffled by the great rifts torn in the side of her car. He wasn't. He knew the marks of a Worm's claws when he saw them. Kirsten died, trapped in her car as water poured in through those slashes.

Because of him. Because he'd failed to protect her.

Bree, not Kirsten, slept beside him. An innocent woman whose life was already unraveling at his touch. He'd ruined her wedding. Driven her from her home. Poisoned the relationship between her and her fiancé.

And now, he'd slept with her, letting himself be seduced by the comfort of her body.

Was there no end to his selfishness?

Untangling himself from her embrace, he tried to slip out of bed unnoticed. But as the mattress shifted, she gave a small purr of pleasure and opened her eyes. "Morning."

So much for his cowardly escape. "Good morning."

No sense trying to be subtle then. He scooped up his pants and pulled them on.

"Where are you going?" Her sleepy eyes, peering through tousled red hair, begged him not to leave. Lie back down, they whispered. Make love to me again. Start the day as my Mate, not a hook up.

Finn ignored those impulses. He'd screwed her life up enough already. "Time for me to meet with the rest of the team working on this problem."

"Gimme a minute. I'll go with you." Cotton sheets slid across her silken curves as she stood, naked and beautiful.

Oh hell, if he didn't leave now, he was going to stay in this bed with her till noon. "It's Flight business," he protested.

Bree planted her hands on her hips, completely unaware of what a delectable pose she struck. "It's *my* land. And *my* problem because of this damned ring."

Hard to argue against that.

A half hour later, they pulled into her driveway. Inside, they found only two people. His Alpha, Brandon Lorde, and Lorde's elderly housekeeper, Amarie, who was puttering in the kitchen.

"Where are all the Hares?" Finn asked. "I'd hoped to introduce Bree to other members of her Kind."

Even first thing in the morning, his Alpha wore a sharp black tailored suit and polished leather shoes. "They're in town. I thought it best for them to stay a little further away, with Cole being hurt and you 'absent.'"

Finn's Dragon bristled at the accusation that lay behind

that word. Where he was last night was his business, not his Alpha's!

Lorde swept past him and offered Bree a hand. "Ms. Williams. Thank you so much for allowing us to base in your house."

"You're welcome to it. I can't stand being alone here anymore. This place needs a Dragon sitting in it."

"Hopefully, we can do something about that. Please, join me at the table. Amarie is preparing breakfast."

Accompanied by the clatter of pans, Finn filled his Alpha in on the night's events. Leaving out, of course, the love they'd shared.

"Do you have any idea what this creature wants, Ms. Williams?"

"He's obsessed with pollution, 'shredding' and vile 'mixings.' It's like he thinks I'm two different things smooshed together."

"Interesting." One of Lorde's long fingers tapped against his coffee cup as he considered that.

"Breakfast!"

Emerging from the kitchen with a pile of plates, Amarie scurried about the table. Rolls, jam, toast, eggs, pancakes, hash browns... despite her age, she darted here and there, distributing a mountain of food.

Clearly, she was a woman used to feeding a full Flight of Dragons! Finn had more than he could eat – and to his amusement, Bree's plate held as much as his and Lorde's combined.

"Ma'am," Bree protested, "I couldn't possibly eat all this."

"Well, you should try. Eat! Eat! You need this!"

Bree caught his eye. He shrugged. Lorde's housekeeper had a reputation for being a few cards short of a deck.

But while the two of them exchanged secret grins, his Alpha frowned. "Explain, if you will, Amarie. Ms. Williams seems quite healthy. Why do you think she requires such nourishment?"

"Well," the old Hare tutted, "she's eating for two now."

Finn's fork slipped through his numb fingers and clattered to the plate. Bree froze like a deer in headlights.

The old woman's eyes darted back and forth between the two of them. "Did you not know that you two... that you had a, um... oh my."

"Amarie...," Lorde sighed.

From deep within his soul, a rumble arose. A thundering, bass howl of purest joy.

Our Mate is with child! We have a family! Ours!

For one second, he shared its delight. Then he realized what this meant, and a tidal wave of rage swept over him as he felt the iron jaws of Fate's snare closing around him.

His damned Dragon wanted a family? Well, nobody had asked him! He didn't choose any of this. Not 'Mate', not 'family.' He was *not* going to be trapped by some stroke of luck.

A threatening growl wove itself into his Dragon's song.

Shut up, you, he told it. *This is your fault.*

"Bree..." Torn between joy and anger, words failed him.

But he didn't need to speak. His expression had already given his doubts away. "Excuse me," she whispered as she staggered to her feet.

Amarie wilted. "I'll be in the kitchen. Cleaning dishes." Damage done, she slunk off in shame.

Leaving him with his annoyed Alpha. "Let's step outside, shall we?" Irritation dripped from every one of Lorde's words.

Why not? Breakfast was ruined. Finn threw his napkin on his plate and followed.

No one said anything as they crossed the lawn and threaded through the towering pines. Only when the eerie mist that hid the Wellspring came into view did the two men slow to a halt.

"Is there something you want to tell me?" Lorde asked.

"Yes!" Finn snapped. "You're not my father. Quit talking to me like I'm some idiot teenager too stupid to use protection."

At that rebellion, a red light flared in his Alpha's eyes. Finn braced himself for his own Dragon's fury. Honestly, he didn't want to challenge Lorde for control of the Flight. Yet, the need to lash out, to break free of the fetters closing in around him, was too strong.

He needn't have worried. His Dragon didn't even stir. Guess it wasn't too pleased with him right now.

And so, to his disgust, he found himself glancing away from Lorde's burning gaze. "Did you? Use protection?"

"It was a mistake, dammit. And bad luck. Stop riding me. It's not like I'm the first member of this Flight to screw up."

That burning stare pinned him in place. "She's your Mate, isn't she?"

"No."

Pain shot through his head at the denial, a piercing bolt that sent sparks flashing across his sight. What the hell? Had his Dragon just *bit* him?

Lorde regarded him with open disbelief. "Do you expect me to believe it's a coincidence that you went tearing off to her room the moment she was in danger? Do *not* treat me like a fool, Donnelly. I have a Mate of my own."

"Yes, I sensed the threat. That doesn't make us Mates."

"Did you share the Rite of Claiming?"

Finn squirmed as his Alpha dragged him toward the obvious, undeniable truth. And he fought him every step of the way. "Yes. That still doesn't make us Mates."

"Yes, it does!" Lorde's bellow echoed through the woods.

"That is *precisely* what it does! That is the entire point of the ritual!"

"I am not Fate's pawn!" Finn roared back. "I get a choice!"

"And what about Ms. Williams? Does she get a choice too?"

"Yes! Dammit, Lorde, she was engaged to another man. She never would have gone through with the Rite if she thought it was real."

Shock finally shut his Alpha up and Finn pressed his advantage. "I've probably ruined her future now. The wedding's off and I doubt she'll be able to fix things with her fiancé. Not when she's carrying another man's child."

Around them, a deep, lifeless silence filled the forest. Every sensible creature had long since fled the ominous fog. "What a mess," Lorde sighed.

"Tell me about it."

"But there is a way to fix it."

Finn knew his Alpha too well to feel any relief at those words. He'd seen the way Lorde tricked his brothers in the Flight. So, all he offered was a noncommittal, "Oh?"

"The past is gone and yes, you've destroyed Ms. Williams' old dreams. So, make new ones with her. Demolishing the past has cleared the way for a beautiful future."

Finn snorted. "That's your advice? Be a good boy. Do what your Dragon tells you. Walk into the trap, it'll be fine!"

"That's not what I'm…"

"Yes, it is!"

A sob broke the stillness. A world of pain melted down into one soft sound.

Bree stood behind them. Tears ran down her face, a sight that drove a dagger through Finn's heart.

Why was she here? What was she doing? A dozen questions sprang into his mind. Yet, the only words to pass his lips were much simpler. "I'm sorry. I'm so, so sorry."

"It's okay." She swatted the tears off her cheeks. Others immediately spilled out. "We agreed, remember? Nobody's trapped. We get to choose."

How hollow those promises sounded now.

"I didn't mean..."

With a wave of her hand, she dismissed his excuses. "Yes, you did. And you're right. This *is* a trap. One you can't escape."

"That's not true." He reached for her, but she backed away. Finn let his hand drop to his side. He'd lost any right to touch her. "We can still choose."

"Really?" Tears choked her laugh. "You think we can walk away from each other now? You think you can let your child grow up, never knowing her father? I don't think you can. I think you're a good man and Fate picked a bait you can't resist."

She was right. Finn hung his head at the truth in her words. Choice was an illusion. He'd thrown it away the moment he decided to go through with the Rite of Claiming.

Lorde cleared his throat. "Ms. Williams, I want to assure you that..."

"Wait, please. Let me say something before I lose my nerve. Finn?" Though her face was stained with tears, her smile remained bright. "I didn't love Daven. I had fun with him – and I was too silly to know the difference. I'm glad we didn't get married. I think I understand love now. It's wanting the best for someone, no matter what the cost to you. Exactly the opposite of what Daven and I had."

Once more, he stepped toward her and once more she retreated.

"I love you." Grief and adoration lit her face. "And I want you to be free."

With that, she stepped backward into the edge of the Wellspring's mist.

"Bree, no!" Finn screamed. Both he and Lorde leaped for her.

And slammed into an invisible wall with bone-jarring force.

The fog curled around her, and she was gone.

The last thing he saw was her eyes, shining with love and tears.

hispers flowed around her. Scraps of mist and fog, coiling and swirling through the greyness.

Then a woman spoke, "Be welcome."

With those words, the endless void vanished.

Bree sat on a neatly trimmed lawn. Not a lump, a speck of dirt, or a single weed marred its perfect surface. Rose bushes circled the clearing. Each plant boasted exactly twelve red blooms, every one flawless and unfaded. A path of white gravel cut through a wall of roses leading to the woods where graceful birches marched off into the distance in neat, orderly lines.

It was beautiful... but kind of creepy in its perfection. Like a neurotic English garden plunked down in the middle of a faerie tree farm.

The people gathered here were as weird as their greenery.

A dozen Adanai clustered close to each other, watching and whispering. Tall, impossibly thin, they wore gauzy white robes. Braided with flowers, the hair of both men and women cascaded all the way to the ground.

And everything was perfect. Hair. Clothes. Features. Nobody had a pimple, a grey hair, or a smudge of dirt on their brilliant clothes.

Bree almost laughed. Put her in one of those gowns and the darned thing would be covered with grass stains in five minutes.

All of the creatures kept their distance, except one. Legs curled under her, a woman sat beside her. Staring into her face with rapt delight.

"Hi!" Bree croaked.

The Adanai flinched, fluttering like startled birds.

That was encouraging. They seemed almost as scared of her as she was of them.

Only her companion showed no fear. "Be welcome," she repeated.

"Thank you. I'm Bree Williams."

"We know you. We observed you."

They must be the white 'ghosts' haunting her kitchen. "Thanks for letting me in here."

"How could we refuse?" Silver eyes like mirror shards studied her. "Your pain and your… 'love'? It is intoxicating."

Okaaay. That wasn't ominous or anything. Bree's heart started to beat faster. "Will the Dragons come through too?"

"No. The way is closed to them."

"Good." So, Step One of her plan had worked. Step Two had been to ask for sanctuary for herself and her child. Yet, after just two minutes in this 'Otherworld' that seemed like a bad idea. Humans could never live this way.

On to Step Three, then. "What's your name?"

"Queen Lilalanandalissattra."

Lila? Sattra? Mangling a queen's name didn't seem wise so Bree fell back on protocol. "Your Majesty, there are other gates here, right? That go back to Earth?"

The queen inclined her head.

"Could you let me through one? I'd like to go back to my own world, but I don't want the Dragons to know about that."

Better if Finn thought her dead. Alive, and he'd spend the rest of his life searching for her. Fate's trap would close around him. He'd blame himself for her 'death', of course. A thought that sickened her. Could she really saddle him with that guilt?

Yes, because the alternative was an eternity tied to a woman he didn't love. Dragons might not be truly eternal, but they lived for centuries at least. True, her 'loss' would hurt him. The pain would fade in time, however, as had all the other griefs of his life. When, at last, he met the right woman, he'd be free to follow his heart.

"No." No explanation. No apologies. Just 'no.'

That word torpedoed a huge hole in Step Three. But years of negotiating assured Bree that there was always a way to get a client to say 'yes.' You just needed to know your customer's goal. "May I ask why you're your Majesty?"

"My Lord has closed the Ways. To open them requires consent from both."

One to close, two to open. Got it. Sounded like this 'Lord' was the cause of the Wellsprings' recent failures.

Maybe she could help Finn's Flight – and herself, at the same time. "Could I petition his Majesty for permission to open the Wellsprings?"

A faint pinch of the lips. The first thing even vaguely close to an emotion to cross the queen's face. "You may. Though, I cannot promise your safety."

Potentially violent clients? Hadn't dealt with that in her years as a negotiator. Still, what other choice did she have? "I'll take that risk."

"Come then." The queen drifted to her feet in one effortless, unbroken glide, as if she'd been lifted by strings. Bree scrambled up in a more ungainly fashion.

A path of mown grass appeared through the woods, a carpet of green winding through the silvery trees. Not a word passed between Bree and the queen as they walked. Two by two, the court trailed behind them, equally still. On and on they passed, in compete silence, through the perfect, elfin landscape.

The more time she spent in this 'Other Side', the less she liked it. It reminded her of a corpse at a funeral. Pretty but dead.

Moments melted together. Without landmarks, without sound, the world blurred. Bree couldn't say how long they walked. Minutes? Days? Finally, however, the path entered a clearing. At its center stood a pavilion of black silk etched with silver design. On a throne beneath it sat a man, the queen's dark reflection. Black hair to counter her white. Clothes as dark as midnight. And when he turned his disapproving gaze upon her, Bree recognized those lightless eyes.

Her shadow monster. The king of the Other Side was the thing trying to 'shred' her.

With a curtsy so deep she swept the ground, the queen addressed him. "Greetings, my Lord. Bree of the Worlds Beneath would petition you." As the king's eyes narrowed, his Lady added, "She enjoys my protection."

"You presume much, my Lady," he replied, in tones as cold as glacial run-off. "Did I not say that the gates to the Other Side were to be closed?"

"I do not believe so, Lord. You forbade anything to pass from our realm to the mortal world. Yet, you did not speak of mortals entering our land."

That was some fine legal hair-splitting. It vexed the king, but Bree admired it.

"And now you wish me to bend my rule and allow this mongrel to return?"

The queen didn't quibble over that term. "I do."

"No. I see your snare. I will not tread upon it."

Snare? Seemed like a straightforward request to Bree. Yet, the tension in the queen's shoulders, her submissive stance, hinted that the king was right. There were things going on here she didn't understand.

And years in negotiation had taught her that that was a lousy bargaining position. Time to change the playing field. Bree cleared her throat. "My Lord, would you grant me permission to speak?"

Wary, he nodded.

First, the flattery. "You know your queen better than me. I don't see a trap – but if you do, I am sure you're right. Could you please explain it to me? I don't want to be anyone's pawn and I can't avoid a snare I can't see."

"A fair request. Your Worlds Beneath have always fascinated my people. In times past, many of the lesser Kind even Shifted down there. Polluting their pure souls with the filth of mortal desires."

Did he mean Shifters? Bree longed to ask, but you never interrupted someone when they were on a roll.

And the king definitely was. "My Queen has been obsessed with the Worlds Beneath ever since our daughter, Amatessandra, mingled herself with your Kind."

Amatessandra… Tess? Tess Morland was the daughter of these creatures?

"Many others of my court share her madness. The source of their fixation is your 'love'." He spat the word out like a rotten piece of corn. "Our love is pure. Reasoned, elevating, sublime."

Sounded 'cold' to Bree. "Whereas our love is messy. The heights of passion mixed with the worst pain and agony a soul can feel. It draws the highest sacrifices from us… and also drives us to commit unspeakable evils."

The King nodded. "It is pollution."

"Or glory. Joy and sorrow are two sides of the same coin. You can't have one without the other. Most humans would say that love's pains make it even sweeter."

"That is my Queen's opinion. Your 'sacrifice' for that Dragon enchanted her. Now, she wishes me to release you, to reward your devotion. If I do, my court will whisper your tale on cold winter nights. Spreading this madness, this pollution."

Well, the good news was, she finally understand his grievance. The bad news was, she didn't know how to fix the problem and still escape this eerie place.

The king, however, had his own ideas. "You, pawn. Do you truly wish to escape this game? Then help me prove my Lady wrong."

Wow, talk about unappealing offers: 'How about walking into *my* snare instead of hers?' But what other choice did she have?

"How would we do that?"

"Let us test your 'love'. If it proves strong and true, I shall allow you to leave the Other Side. If it is false, you remain here. Or, if you wish, I shall rend the Hares from yourself and your child and cast your mortal bodies back to the Worlds Beneath."

Shivers swept over her, welling up from her Hare. The thought of being trapped here, again, terrified it.

"What exactly is this test?"

"You will see." Cold, glittering eyes studied her.

Could she pass such a test? Two days ago, she didn't even believe in love. Now…

Now, she knew. How it felt to give yourself, wholly, to a man. The joy that came from sacrificing for someone else.

The peace, the confidence that had swept over her as she stepped into the Mist. Knowing that, no matter what happened to her, Finn would be spared.

That was love. Not the half-hearted, lukewarm 'love' of the Other Side. Passion and devotion, the highest emotions humans could feel.

Hell yeah, she loved Finn. And her love could beat any test!

Still, a good negotiator knew when to toss out a counter-offer.

Let's see how much he wants to prove his Lady wrong.

Bree sighed and shook her head. "Without knowing the test, I can't say. Who knows what could go wrong? I could die."

The king leaned forward. Excellent – it meant he was eager. "Yet, this is your only chance. I will not allow you to leave otherwise."

"Staying here doesn't seem *that* bad..." It did. However, the King of the Other Side could never guess how creepy his little 'paradise' was to a human.

Hemming and hawing, she gave him a minute to stew. Then she tossed out the bait. "How about sweetening the deal? If I pass, you agree to allow magic to flow through the Wellsprings again."

He reared back, offended. "Why should I take such a risk?"

"It's only a risk if you think there's a chance I'll pass your test." Bree gave him her sweetest smile.

One long, elegant finger tapped on the arm of his throne as he pondered that. Bree waited, expressionless.

"Very well. I accept your condition. Do you submit to the test?"

"If I pass, you let me leave and allow magic to flow

through the Wellsprings again. If I fail, I remain here. Or go home in pieces."

The king nodded.

"Sounds good. I accept and submit to your test."

Murmurs of delight swept through the watching Adanai. It looked like nothing this exciting had happened on the Other Side since... well, probably since Princess Tess ran away.

Her Hare was a tiny bundle of nerves, shivering endlessly.

Calm down. You're spooking me, and I need to think, okay?

Waves of fear sank to ripples. Guess that was the best her Shifter soul could do.

Once more, she thought of Finn. His pride in himself and his Flight. How much the Wellsprings meant to them all.

This would be her final gift to him. To all of the Shifter world.

The joy of that settled even her skittish Hare. Calm and confident, Bree took a breath and faced the king.

A slow, gloating smirk twisted his handsome face. Now that she'd consented to his test, he didn't bother to hide his contempt for her.

"Let us begin, then," he said.

The Other Side vanished, and she appeared at her lover's bedside.

Daven's bedside.

Not Finn's.

CHAPTER 15

"Whoa! Wait! Stop!" Bree yelled.

Her cry woke Daven. With a squawk, he sat up, eyes darting between her and the dark King who stood beside her. "What the hell?"

"This is *not* a fair test! I don't love him!"

"And yet, you pledged your life to him. You still wear the mark of that vow."

That damnable engagement ring!

"Only because I can't take it off," she snapped. "Which I'm starting to think is your doing."

Daven rubbed his eyes. When that didn't make the two interlopers disappear, he groaned. "I'm dreaming. I have to be dreaming."

"Think of it that way if you wish." The king raised his hand with languid grace. Then his fist snapped shut, as if he grabbed some unseen fly.

Pain tore through Bree. She fell to her knees, sparks of light flooding her vision. Everything – love, fear, thought itself – disappeared, washed away by that agony.

When it dimmed to mere pain, she glanced up, panting.

The king held a rabbit by the scruff of its neck. No, not a rabbit. A Hare, tied to her by a thin, silvery cord.

Her Hare! Her *soul*!

"Did you think that death was the worst that could happen?" Turning to the dazed lawyer, the king explained, "This is the source of your problem."

"A rabbit is the reason my fiancée left me for another guy. Riiight." Daven rolled his eyes. Bree could sympathize.

"Think of it as a symbol. Is your woman a rabbit?"

"No. She's a wolf. A killer," he said sadly.

Once, that would have pleased her. Now, she knew how hollow those things were. Better to be a Hare, a creature of intuition and insight, than an unfeeling competitor.

A black dagger appeared in the king's left hand. He offered it, hilt first, to Daven. "This creature, this weakness, has polluted your woman. Destroy it and she will be yours once again. She will become the woman you knew and loved once more."

"Daven, don't! That's my soul!"

He turned the knife back and forth in his hand. Gingerly, as if he feared it might bite him. "You're not a rabbit, Bree. You're stronger than that."

"Look, I love this thing. It makes me whole. For the first time in my life, I'm happy."

"Without me." His grip on the knife firmed.

"Please don't hurt it," she begged.

He glanced at the king and the squirming Hare he held. "I think he, uh, may be right. You're probably better off without that thing."

And *with* him? No!

Screw the king and screw this unfair 'test.' Bree threw herself toward her Hare…

…and nothing happened. The air turned to molasses around her, cementing her in place.

"Daven, please no! That Hare means everything to me!"

Wrong thing to say! Her ex-fiancé's eyes narrowed dangerously. "Well, maybe it shouldn't. Maybe you'd still love me without it."

How had she ever thought she could marry such a selfish bastard? "Don't *my* desires matter? They would to Finn Donnelly!"

Daven ignored her. "She'll forget him, right?"

The king nodded and held out the kicking Hare.

Shit! Time to try another tactic. "Seriously, Daven? You're going to stab a rabbit? You'll get blood all over yourself!"

"Oh, ugh." Nose wrinkling, Daven recoiled in disgust. He always was the fastidious sort.

"Are you so dainty that you cannot slay a Hare?" Shocked by the lawyer's revulsion, the Adanai shook his head. "And you think yourself a predator."

"Uh…"

"Blood everywhere." Bree threw her arms wide. "And it's going to scream. Did you know rabbits scream? They do. It's horrible. Sounds like a dying child."

"Is this not a mere dream?" the king thundered. "Can you not at least *dream* of being a man and reclaiming your woman?"

Hopefully not! "That's right, this is a dream. You, Daven, are dreaming that if you sacrifice a bunny I'll come back to you. In what world does that make any sense? Damn, you need therapy. This is pathetic. What would the guys in the office think if they could see you now? Daven Kane – Bunny Slayer!"

"And now, I'm getting nagged in my dreams." Rolling his eyes in disgust, Daven tossed the dagger aside and flopped back against his pillow. "Dammit, this is ridiculous!"

As soon as the knife hit the floor, the bedroom vanished. Once more, Bree and the king stood in the gardens of the

Other Side. Around them, the members of the Court chattered in their musical tongue. Several ducked their heads to her. Seemed like she had the audience's favor.

But she *didn't* have her soul. Bree rounded on the king, who still held her struggling Hare. "Give her back!"

His grip tightened, sending darts of pain shooting through her chest. "Restrain yourself. You did not pass that test. Even you must agree that cowardice is not love."

"Well the 'test' was rigged." To her relief, his grip loosened when she stepped back and once more, the agony faded. "You know I don't love Daven."

A rustle of silk on grass announced that the queen had glided up behind her. "One might think, my Lord, that you fear a fair contest."

Once again, Bree was glad to have her on *her* side.

The reprimand stung him, and his eyes narrowed. "Very well. You shall have your 'fair' test. I do not ask your consent, Lady, for what comes next. You have already proven that is not necessary."

The king raised his left hand – and suddenly, out of nowhere, Finn staggered into the clearing.

CHAPTER 16

*A*gain.

Head down, feet tearing ruts in the soft earth, Finn threw himself forward. His Dragon poured its strength into his mortal body, holding nothing back. Power surged, the veins in his neck stood out with the strain. Every muscle in his body twisted, reached the tearing point…

Yet, he went nowhere. The mist surrounding the Wellspring resisted his assault. Soft as cotton, thin as smoke.

And completely impenetrable.

Gasping, he staggered back to the edge of the trees. "Again."

Once more. This time would be different. This time, he'd break through.

"Finn?"

Tess Morland limped out from the woods. Her Mate, Darian, held her elbow, alert to any threat.

"You shouldn't be here," Finn rasped.

"Five minutes after the Adanai hurt Tess, I was on my way to the airport. Finn, listen." Darian grabbed him by the elbow, but he jerked away. "You've been banging your head against this thing for a day now. You've got to stop."

"I can't."

His eyes flickered to Tess. Darian caught his silent question at once and bowed his head. He, too, knew that no Dragon could ever rest while his Mate was in danger.

Tess, however, didn't grasp just how stubborn Dragons could be. "C'mon Big Guy, take a break. If we could just kick our way into the Other Side, we'd be there already. It's going to take more than just brute strength to get through."

"Fine." He called on his Dragon for another run. "You work on the 'more.' I'll keep trying the brute strength."

"Finn..."

"Again!" His Dragon's roar joined his as he charged forward, tensed for an impact...

...that never came.

The unbreakable wall melted into fog and Finn went sprawling into the Other Side.

HE HIT THE GROUND ROLLING.

Keen Dragon senses and years of battle laid the field plain to him even as he leaped to his feet.

Garden full of Adanai, screaming in horror and fleeing.

Not threats. Ignore.

Bree.

Unharmed. Ignore.

Guy in black holding a dagger to Bree's Hare.

Target acquired.

Magic swirled around him, weaving the world together. Each draught of air he drew filled his body with its intoxicating richness. Pure oxygen for the fire of his Dragon soul. Finn gave himself to that wild power. As his Dragon's might poured into him, he crouched and prepared to tear the Other Side apart for kidnapping his Mate.

Alone among his people, the black-clad stranger didn't even flinch. "Shift and the Hare dies."

With razor sharp precision, Finn froze. His Dragon screamed in outrage. Fast and lethal, it *knew* it could kill that creature before he hurt Bree.

Maybe. Probably. But we're not taking that risk.

Hissing with fury, his Dragon sank back. Coiled and ready for his call. Its fire burned in Finn's eyes.

"Good. How pleasant to learn that you can control yourself. Now we can speak."

Just keep thinking that, buddy. I don't need a Dragon to snap your neck.

"Bree? You okay?" He inched closer to her. Testing to see how near he could get to his true target, the guy with her Hare.

"Yeah. Rattled, but fine. I… Finn, I'm so sorry."

"No closer," the Adanai ordered.

Okay, so the guy wasn't a complete idiot. Too bad. And what the hell was that strange, pale cord tying Bree to her Hare? "Who's the jerk?" he asked her.

"The king of this place. I think he's Tess' father."

Killing Tess' dad could make Flight gatherings awkward.

Oh well. He'd deal with that problem when it arose. The SOB shouldn't have hurt his Mate. "All right, Mr. Everlyn."

The Adanai frowned. Wasn't 'Everlyn' Tess' maiden name?

If so, her dad didn't seem to recognize it. Finn decided to keep using it anyways, since it annoyed the bastard. "Here's what's going to happen. You're gonna let go of that Hare. Then Bree and I are walking back to the Wellspring and we're returning to our world. You don't attack us, and I won't set your little Enchanted Forest on fire. Everybody happy, nobody gets hurt. Sound good?"

"The doors and gates are closed to you. So they shall remain – until you pass the test."

"What test?"

Despite her bravado, he heard a quaver in Bree's voice. "The king is trying to convince his wife there's no such thing as true love. So far, all he's managed to prove is that Daven and I don't like each other much. And, frankly, that Daven doesn't love anyone except himself."

Only six feet separated him from that arrogant prick. Six feet. He could cross that in the blink of an eye. Snap the bastard's arm before he could even twitch.

Couldn't he? His Dragon believed it. So did he.

But something in the Adanai's face held him back. A hint of eagerness, as if he hoped the Dragon would attack.

A good warrior trusted his instincts. Finn forced himself to wait. "Look, buddy, I don't know what's going on between you and the misses. But I don't intend to jump through any hoops for you. Screw you and your test."

"Then you will remain here, with this woman, for all time."

A slight flare of the nostrils betrayed his eagerness. Oh yeah. The SOB was trying to goad him into losing his temper. "Let me get this straight. If I don't pass your test, I will be forced to live forever in a faerie paradise with the woman I love?"

Love.

There. He'd said it. And it hadn't been anywhere near as hard to admit as he'd feared.

"Yes."

"You need to up your threat game, bro. That's not a scary prospect."

Now the creature did smile, a thin-lipped, arrogant

smirk. "For you, perhaps. However, the child she carries will not fare as well. Mortals do not thrive here. What crawls from her womb will not be human."

A fine red mist settled across his sight as Bree choked back a whimper. This thing dared to threaten his unborn child? Blood drummed in his ears as rage set his heart racing. His Dragon crouched, begging him to Shift and loose it upon their enemy.

Not yet. He still has my Mate's soul.

Humor was his shield, the only thing keeping him from going berserk. "Attaboy. 'Pass my test or your child suffers' is a much better threat." As anger lit the Adanai's eyes, a vicious joy flashed through Finn. Somebody didn't like getting mocked, at all. "Here's my counter-threat. You can't hold a knife to that Hare's throat forever. Sooner or later, you'll have to put it down. And when you do, I'll tear you to pieces. So how about you let us go, now, and nobody has to die?"

The king waved the Hare's limp body back and forth. Only its rolling eyes proved it was still alive. "Is this all that holds you back from slaying me? Then let us dispense with it."

With a flick of his wrist, he tossed the Hare into Bree's arms. Her Shifter soul melded into her body as she caught it.

That was all the invitation Finn needed. He pounced on the Adanai, grabbing the wrist of his knife-hand with an iron grip. Triumphant, his Dragon urged him to Shift, to rend this villain to pieces and...

Calm, unworried, the king studied him.

"Drop the knife!" Finn growled.

"Take it. You're going to need it."

He grabbed it – not because he believed the guy. But Tess claimed the Adanai had Dragon-slaying weapons. Maybe this was one of them. "Now open the Wellspring and let us out."

"No. You have not passed my test."

Bree hurried to his side, tremors shaking her lithe form. Gently, he pushed her behind him. "Hang on, babe. I'll get us out of here. You." He shook the king like a terrier with a rat. "You think I won't kill you?"

"I know you won't." That sneer was really getting on his nerves! "I am the only one who can open the Wellsprings. Kill me and your child pays the price."

"Death isn't the worst thing you need to worry about," Finn growled.

An actual flash of happiness lit the jerk's bony face. "I am pleased you know this. Your Lady seemed quite unaware of that fact."

"Let us go or I will hurt you. Badly." To emphasize the point, he squeezed the man's delicate wrist.

"And how do you plan to do that?"

In his hand, the bones of the king's arm melted away. The skin twisted like taffy, then tore. With a gentle 'plop' his hand fell to the ground.

Finn jerked back in shock.

The Adanai raised the stump of his wrist. Tendrils of dark mist rose from it, forming fingers, then skin that paled to ivory white. A second later, he held aloft a new hand.

Without a single wince of pain. "I am the Lord of this realm. You are a mere trespasser. You cannot harm me."

Free me, his Dragon demanded. *I will teach him differently.*

Can you do that without killing him?

Irritation and silence.

I take it that's a 'no'.

Bree snuggled close to him. Feeling her heart beat against his arm, Finn's stomach roiled with impotent fury. He couldn't risk her and their unborn child. That only left him one option: play along. "So, what's your test?"

"Prove that true love exists."

"Fine." If that was what was needed, so be it. "Let her go. Keep me here."

"Finn, no! I won't leave you!"

God, he loved her. Her sweet but foolish devotion. "Bree, listen. It's not just you. You've got to take care of the baby."

"I can't live without you! I won't!"

How many times had he thought that in his long life? How many times had Fate taught him how much suffering people could endure? "You feel that now. But you'll have our child, and…"

"Stop! Stop!" the king wailed.

To Finn's surprise, the Adanai seemed genuinely distraught. He fanned his hand furiously, as if their words smelled like rotting fish.

"Cease this idiocy at once! This is agitation, not love. No one doubts that your whims madden you to the edge of self-destruction."

The Dragon drew himself to his full, towering height. "In our world, sacrificing yourself to save another is considered the highest expression of love."

"Not when you wish to die."

Cold, beetle-black eyes locked with his. In a droning hiss, the king laid bare the shame that festered at the center of Finn's life. Baring his dishonor for his Mate to see.

"Yes, you wish to die. Life has grown tedious for you. You will not raise a weapon against yourself, for that is a craven's path. Instead, you throw yourself into battle, over and over, and are disappointed anew each time you fail to find the escape you seek.

"Now, you have fallen into love's trap once more. You dream that this time it will triumph. Yet, in your heart, you know this 'love' will fail, as all the others have. Thus, you hope to die, to spare yourself the pain of seeing your passion destroyed. And you have the cheek, the impudence to stand before me and swear that your cowardice proves your devotion."

Each word was a hammer's blow against his heart, shaking him to his core. This was the ugly truth, the rot that infested every aspect of his life like a thick, black mold. He couldn't live without love – but he couldn't trust it, either. Stunned, speechless, he felt the last of his Dragon's power drain away.

Until a soft tug at his arm drew him back from that precipice.

Bree hugged him. Anger had slain her terror, leaving nothing except a fierce, defiant love. "That isn't true. He doesn't know anything about you!"

Finn swallowed, daunted by the king's cold smile. "Yeah, he does. I don't know how, but he hit the nail on the head."

"No. He hit your fears on the head."

How could she defend him – after he had spurned her and their child? If he'd been a man, a true Dragon, none of them would be in this mess. "Babe, I'm a coward."

"You're a brave man who's afraid of being coward. There's a difference."

"I abandoned you." The words escaped in a harsh croak.

The love in her eyes never dimmed. "You're here now, aren't you? Yeah, you made a mistake. But you came back."

He didn't deserve such love.

Yet, unworthy as he was, she'd given it to him. That fact, that blessing, pierced the despair that threatened to choke him. Peace followed it, and a calm certainty.

He wasn't the man she thought he was. But he *was* the man who was going to save her.

Throwing his shoulders back, he faced the King of the Adanai. "All right, Mr. Everlyn. I'm tired of playing Twenty

Questions. Name your proof and I'll give it to you. If you don't want me to die for Bree, what *do* you want?"

"Live for her."

"Isn't that what I'm trying to do?" Finn grumbled. "Let us go back to Earth and I'll live for her. I'll Claim her truly and be her Dragon. If she'll have me," he added, shaken by a sudden doubt.

Bree beamed at him, proud and sure. "Oh, she'll have you, all right."

"Charming," the king sniffed. "Then go. I've given you what you need to return." He pointed a graceful finger at Finn's right hand.

The one that held the black knife.

"What happened to 'death is not the answer'?"

Openly gloating now, the Adanai almost purred. "No one need die. The Other Side shuns the Worlds Beneath. Were you purely mortal, you would naturally fall back to your world. But you are not pure, are you? You are muddled. Drive the blade into yourself; it will not harm you. Cut away the pollution and set yourself free."

The outline of the trap was becoming plain. "By pollution, you mean our Shifter souls. My Dragon. Her Hare."

"Yes. Don't worry. They will not die. But they *will* remain here, forever."

"Let me get this straight. You want me to sever my soul – and the soul of my *Mate*. And somehow, you think this will prove true love exists?"

Beside him, Bree frowned, clutching his arm. Even his Dragon rocked back on its heels, baffled, as he struggled to understand this madman.

"Cleansed of its ties to the Other Side, mortal flesh sinks to the Worlds Beneath like a stone." His soft words slithered through the air, sly as a serpent in the grass. "Dragging anything it touches with it."

Dragging…?

There. That was the test. He saw it clearly now.

"I don't understand," Bree murmured.

He did.

So did his Dragon. He felt it, felt its boundless love for its Mate. Knew that there was no sacrifice too great for its heart.

Silently, it bowed its head. Finn sent his Dragon one last, silent thanks for the joy it had brought into his life.

Then he pulled his Mate close, holding her tight against his body with one hand.

With the other, he drove the black blade into his stomach.

Pain slashed through him, a stroke of icy cold. Roaring, his Dragon appeared beside him. A thin silver cord, severed by the knife's stroke, trailed behind it as it launched itself into the pale skies of the Other Side. As it rose, leaving him forever, Finn felt himself falling. Backward, down, into the mists.

With Bree in his arms, he surrendered himself to that fall.

CHAPTER 17

hispers filled Bree's house again. Not the mutterings of curious Adanai, spying from the edges of the world. No, these voices were more mundane. Hares, Dragons, and other Shifters, trying to make sense of the day's events.

Finn was fine. Unharmed, physically.

But he wasn't a Dragon. He'd lost his Shifter soul.

Beer in hand, he sat outside, staring blindly at the sunset. His Flight avoided him. Even his Alpha. Bree wanted to scream at them, "It's not contagious! Don't shun him! He did this for me!"

The worst part? Nothing else had changed. Daven's ring still clung to her finger like a barnacle. That impenetrable mist still blocked off the Wellspring.

Which meant that somehow, they hadn't 'passed' the Dark King's test.

Bree sent a venomous thought in the bastard's direction.

How could this not be proof? What more *do you want us to sacrifice?*

122

The greatest act of love she had ever seen… and it wasn't 'good' enough.

Dammit, her house was as quiet as a funeral home! Bree stomped into the kitchen, elbowed her way through the crowd, and grabbed herself a beer as well. Then she stormed back out, scattering bemused Dragons, and plunked herself down beside Finn.

"Hey."

"Hello, Bree."

"Stop that!" she begged.

"Stop what?"

"Being 'polite.' Good evening, Ms. Williams," she warbled in her best professional tone. "How are you on this fine day?"

The joke didn't tease a smile from him. Still wrapped in stony grief, he sighed. "How am I supposed to greet you?"

"Like this." She slipped an arm around his big waist and snuggled closer. "Or this." A kiss on the chin. "Or…"

He snorted. Not a laugh, but better than nothing. "You shouldn't drink that. You're pregnant, remember?"

"There you go. That greeting works too!" She grinned at him – then took a sip.

"Bree…"

"One beer is not going to hurt the kid. Then I'll be good. I promise."

The conversation died out. The two of them sat, sipping their drinks. Offering the wordless comfort of their bodies.

When the beers ran out, Bree broke the silence. "How do you feel?"

"Empty. Numb. The world isn't bright anymore." Then he shook his head. "Listen to me whine. Sorry. I'll be fine. Don't worry."

Would he? Could anyone be 'fine' with half a soul? "I asked. You're not whining."

"Mmm." Now he did inch away.

Bree held tight and refused to let him escape. "Okay, this is just grim. I need to cheer you up. Let's do something fun."

"Fun." Bitterness dripped from that word. "Bree, I don't feel like doing anything. I'm tired."

"No, you're depressed. That's different. You *need* something to snap you out of this funk."

Every muscle in his body tensed. Again, he tried to pull away.

She didn't let him.

"I don't think this is the sort of thing that can be cured by a nice movie."

"Mmm… probably not," she agreed. "What about a wedding? Would a wedding cheer you up?"

"What?" Now she had his attention. "Who's getting married?"

"We could. Tonight. Right here, right now."

Before he could laugh at her and make her lose her nerve, Bree dropped to one knee in front of him. "Finn Donnelly, I love you. Before I met you, I didn't even know what that word meant. Now I do, and I can't imagine living without you. I want you beside me for the rest of my life. I want you to help me raise the child we brought into this world. Will you marry me?"

He didn't answer. Just stared at her in shock, like she'd ripped her blouse off in public.

"I know this isn't traditional and I don't have a ring to offer you," she teased, "unless you can yank this thing off my finger."

"Bree…"

"But I'm serious. Please, marry me." She scooped up one of his big hands in hers. Trying to ignore Daven's stupid ring.

Shame brightened his eyes as he turned away. "I'm not a Dragon anymore."

"So? You're still a man. Which *is*, after all, what I always expected to marry. Remember, until a week ago, I didn't even know Dragons existed."

He still wouldn't face her. "You deserve better."

"Oh, so Shifters are better, are they?" She kissed his fingers, wishing with all her heart that he would look into her eyes and see how much she loved him. "Didn't you say that your Alpha's Mate is human? Did he marry down?"

"No! No, no, no! That's not what I'm…" The shock of her words did exactly what she'd hoped. He glanced her way… and hesitated, caught by the adoration he saw.

Still, he coughed up one last lame objection. "This is different."

"Oh, I see. So, guy-Shifters can marry mortal women, but girl-Shifters can't marry mortal men? Is that what you're saying?"

"No, I…" His nose wrinkled in a most adorable way.

"Then tell me this: do you love me?"

"Yes." Soft as a sigh, but still clear.

She lowered his hands to her belly. Still flat but holding the promise of new life. "Do you want to be a father?"

"Oh, yes." The yearning in those two words said far more than any speech.

"Then will you marry me?"

Bree's stomach twisted in a knot as he hesitated. How the hell did guys find the nerve to ask this question?

Locked in thought, he hesitated, head hung low. Her worries turned to fears as seconds ticked past. Was he still too hurt to trust love again? Then three words set her whole world right.

"Yes. I will."

She laughed with sheer delight. "Oh damn, Finn! What took you so long to decide? You scared me half to death!"

With a chuckle, he raised her hands to his lips for a kiss –

and Daven's oversized engagement ring promptly bopped him on the nose.

"That thing has to go," he growled.

"I wish."

Finn tugged at it… and the ring popped off in his hand.

"What the…!"

Her shriek of delight brought the rest of his Flight spilling out of the house. "We passed! We passed his stupid test!"

Finn chucked the ring over his shoulder and swept her into his arms. His lips met hers in a kiss that proclaimed his love and passion more richly than any words. When it broke, she leaned against him, breathless and aching for more.

"I love you," he whispered.

"I know. And I guess even the King of the Other Side knows it too."

"And if he does…" Finn bolted to his feet, dragging her with him. "Lorde! If that Adanai kept his promise, the Wellsprings should be returning."

Like an army heading to war, his Flight swept out across the lawn. "On it," Lorde snapped.

Until Bree's squawk of horror halted all the Dragons in their tracks. "Finn Donnelly, did you throw that ring away?"

"Yes. You didn't want to keep it, did you?"

"Do you have any idea how much that thing cost?" she wailed.

"Uh, no. A lot?"

Chuckles spread among his Flight. Bree waved them off. "You guys go. I'll find it."

"Given your role in these events," Lorde protested, "I believe you should accompany us."

"No, I've got to find that thing. Daven will *sue* me."

The back door popped open and Amarie, Lorde's housekeeper, trotted out – holding aloft a large bent twig. "Not to worry, miss. I've got a stick. You go on. I'll find your ring."

"With a stick?" The old lady was sweet but crazy.

"With a dowsing rod." Finn grinned and tugged her toward his waiting Flight.

This time, she didn't complain.

CHAPTER 18

In the gloom of early evening, the pool glittered with a silvery light, as if a million tiny pearls bubbled in its waters. Her Wellspring was back. Free from those haunting mists and fully alive. A soft breeze that only a Witch Hare could sense swirled up from it. Bree felt her Hare lean forward, sniffing at the magic-rich current which washed over its whiskers and fur.

Lorde and Darian Morland, the two Dragons present, took point. The rest of them hung back until the Alpha gave the all-clear sign.

"Ms. Noonan? Your assessment?"

The senior Witch Hare bustled forward. Finn and Bree curled up under a pine at the edge of the woods and watched the woman work her mojo. Bree's own Hare twitched with curiosity.

I bet you think this is a lot more interesting than real estate!

Sniff… snuffle… sniff, sniff, sniff. Whiskers tickled up and down her spine. Yup. A career change seemed likely. At least, if her Shifter soul had anything to say about it.

"Confirmation, Mr. Lorde," the lead Witch called. "Gates are once more open. Energy levels restored. Elevated, in fact. There's a tremendous inflow of magic!"

Finn gave her shoulders a squeeze. "Well, Tess' dad might be a dick, but at least he's an honest dick."

"I bet he's a sore loser, though. Glad I'm not on the Other Side right now!"

Down by the pool, the Dragons finished their circuit. Lorde nodded. "Excellent. Morland, I want you to remain here while the Hares complete their…"

"Incoming!" the other Dragon roared.

A geyser of mist erupted from the pool, covering its surface, once more, with a thick fog.

The air around Lorde and Morland exploded in shimmering lights and suddenly, two Dragons – black and gold – crouched by the water's edge. The Hares threw themselves flat in the long grass. A moment later, six panicked bunnies came zigzagging out of the clearing, bolting for the deep woods.

Finn surged to his feet. He straightened, drew a breath…

…and blushed with shame when nothing happened. Though, when Bree scrambled up, he still stepped gallantly between her and this new threat.

From the mist stepped a familiar form. A slender, graceful Lady dressed in flowing robes and flower garlands.

"Hold up!" Finn barked. "Morland, that's your mother-in-law!"

The gold Dragon's head snapped back. Then slowly, carefully, it leaned down and sniffed her.

The queen permitted this, as if a large dog – not a Dragon – sought her scent. When Morland pulled back, she glided up the gentle hill toward the woods.

And Bree and Finn.

"Lady." Finn gave her a curt nod.

With a serene smile, she said, "You have my gratitude. An ancient argument is now settled."

"You'll forgive us if we're not overjoyed." Arm linked through her man's, Bree stood beside him. "Your 'victory' cost my Mate his Dragon soul."

Her anger didn't disturb the White Lady at all. "That is why I have come. To repay that debt."

"Are you not listening? He lost his *soul*. No amount of compensation pay will make up for that!"

"Bree." Finn squeezed her hand. Didn't do a thing to cheer her up, but she took the hint and fell silent.

"Walk with me." Without checking to see if they followed, she retraced her path back down to the pool. Hesitantly, the lovers followed. At its edge, the queen paused. "Look into the waters. You will see what others saw in ancient times."

That was his 'reward'? A history lesson? Bree bit back a sharp retort.

Tossed and stirred by springs welling up from deep in the earth, the water bubbled away as he drew even closer.

"What do you see?" the Lady asked Finn.

"Not much."

"Look deeper, then."

Finn knelt for a closer look. Unhappy, Bree folded her arms across her chest. The presence of the two Dragons, towering overhead, gave her some comfort. If the Adanai were up to new tricks, Lorde and Morland would put a quick stop to them.

Light and musical, the queen's speech was almost a song. "In ancient times, our people gazed through these doorways. Not the Adanai; we remained pure. Yet, the mortal worlds drew the lesser races like moths to a flame. Intoxicating above all things was your 'love.' Dragons, Bears, Wolves...

even Rats longed for it. Enough that, despite my Lord's commands, many Shifted here."

"Is that why the Wellsprings died? You closed the gates to stop more souls from joining us?" Finn didn't look up from the waters as he spoke.

"Yes. But the wells are open again. What was done before may be done anew." The edges of the queen's form blurred, growing misty and vague. "I can say no more on this matter. I pray I do not need to."

In ancient day, Dragons Shifted here...

The ways are open again.

What was done before...

"Finn!" Bree gasped and dropped to her knees beside him. Her move brought a smile to the queen's face as the Adanaie faded completely away.

Love draws them, like moths to a flame.

Bree pressed her face against Finn's shoulder. She felt the lines of his muscles, hard against her soft cheek and reveled in the musky, male scent of his body. This was the man she loved. The father of her child. Her lover. Her protector. She cherished every facet of him, from the gruff warrior to the quiet watcher. She let that adoration fill her, savoring its pains and its joys.

And somewhere on the Other Side, something moved. White, frosted, a shape grew in the twisting depths of the pool.

"Bree, I see..."

"So do I."

A Dragon's face appeared in the waters. Scarred by battle, the light of its blue eyes dimmed by the weight of sacrifice. Yet, the touch of their love still summoned it to gaze once more, as it had centuries ago, at the wonders of the Worlds Beneath.

Finn held his hand out over the image, inches above the

bubbling water. "What do you say, old boy? Willing to give love another shot?"

Its nostrils flared, uncertain.

"You never fail till you stop trying," Bree whispered.

Another sniff – and then it launched itself forward. Water sprayed high into the air. Light, not a Dragon, burst forth. Sparkling above the pool, swirling around her… then raining down upon Finn.

Cold blue fire blazed to life in her lover's eyes. Finn gasped, rocking back on his heels. Around him, a serpentine image that only Shifters could see flickered to life again.

Finn was a Dragon once more.

Tears of joy ran down her face as she threw herself into his arms. Laughing, he kissed her. Shifting back to human form, Lorde and Morland trotted over to join the celebration. Back slaps and congratulations rained down.

When the tumult died, Bree peered up into her lover's beaming face. "Ready for that marriage?"

"Nope."

Once, that would have worried her. Now, no doubts remained. Finn loved her. Even the Lord of the Adanai knew that. "Don't tell me you've changed your mind?" she laughed.

"Of course not, silly. But you don't need to cheer me up anymore. And you deserve a proper wedding. Let's take it slow and do this thing right, shall we?"

A real wedding. With gowns and bridesmaids and a honeymoon.

That sounded wonderful.

"Well, I cleared New Year's Eve," she reminded him. "How about then?"

Pride and joy lit his craggy face and he kissed her once again. "New Year, new life."

* * *

Thank you for reading Dragon's Redemption! We hope you loved it! If you did then we are pretty sure you are going to love the next book in the series, Dragon Renegade!

<u>Click here to get Dragon Renegade on Amazon!</u>

How about a little preview of Dragon Renegade ...

HOW MUCH THE WORLD COULD CHANGE IN EIGHT HOURS...

Head spinning, Maya Graham smoothed her dress. It was her favorite, a cheery yellow sundress that showed off her long legs and tanned shoulders. After you cleaned up from a three-mile run on a hot Florida day, it was just the thing to keep cool.

That was her main concern when she put it on this morning.

Then, her boss, Lucian Fowler, called from New York. On a Saturday. He needed to talk to her, now. Not over the phone – in person. No, not tomorrow. Now. As in, a car would pick her up momentarily. That car whisked her to a private airport where a small chartered jet hustled her to New York City and dumped her into a waiting limo. Which, in turn, rocketed through Manhattan traffic to deliver her to the posh New Amsterdam Tower.

That was how she came to be sitting here, in the Tower, with its polished marble floors, watching bankers and investors stalk past in suits and designer gowns, wearing a dress as out of place as a dandelion in a mausoleum. Struggling not to shiver in the Tower's artic air conditioning.

And why so much hurry, anyway? Maya was an archeologist, not a stock broker. Pre-contact Native American Ethnography fascinated her... but even she had to admit it wasn't a time-sensitive field.

A black-clad valet appeared at her elbow. "Ms. Graham? Mr. Fowler will see you now."

"Of course." She followed him, her sandals whisper-quiet on the hall's stone floor. A tiny elevator flitted up thirty floors and opened to reveal a long corridor covered in Turkish silk carpets. Pedestals lined it, each one holding some priceless relic. Egyptian curse tablets. Roman busts. A brilliant jeweled egg that was either a Faberge – or a remarkable fake. And good heavens, was that a 17th century English witch-bottle? Each new wonder held her for a moment, like a fly on syrup.

"Ahem." The valet frowned at the distance opening between them. With a blush, Maya rushed to catch up.

The hallway opened onto a corner office. Floor to ceiling windows offered a breathtaking view of Central Park. In the midst of them, with his hands folded behind his back, stood Lucian Fowler.

Three years she'd worked for the American Prehistoric Ethnography Project, and in all that time, she'd never actually seen her boss. An APEP agent had hired her. Lucian was older than he sounded on the phone – and much more handsome. Age had scattered flecks of grey through his glossy brown hair, but it had not added weight to his sculpted waist or weakened the powerful muscles that moved beneath his red silk shirt as he turned to welcome her.

"Ms. Graham. How good of you to come."

His eyes lingered on her tanned legs and Maya felt warmth creep onto her cheeks. "Thank you for sending the plane. I'm sorry I didn't have a chance to change into something more appropriate."

"Oh, you're fine." He chuckled, his eyes crawling up and down her thighs. "In fact, I wouldn't complain at all if you wore something even more 'inappropriate.'"

Forget the business suit. Now she wished she was wearing a burka. With an awkward smile, Maya took a chair. And tugged her dress as low as it would go.

Lucian settled down on the other side of the desk, which ended the ogling. "You're probably curious why you're here."

"Yes, sir. I hope there isn't a problem with the Amesfield dig."

"No problem at all." Locking his hands together, he spun lazily back and forth. "Quite the opposite. We are delighted with the work you've done for APEP. With just scraps of data, you managed to locate the first Ais and Mayaca settlements in Florida. The Amesfield dig, in particular, is going to expand our knowledge of these tribes a hundred fold."

Pride welled up, squashing the butterflies of doubt that had troubled her all the way up from Florida. "That's so kind of you. And thank you, sir, for the generous funding. It was an archeologist's dream."

"Oh, you haven't seen 'generous' yet."

Why did that sound ominous? Maya scolded herself for being paranoid.

"We're moving you off the Amesfield project."

"What? But sir! We've only excavated one residence. There's so much more to do!"

"And someone else will do it. Don't worry."

But not her? Baffled, Maya bit her lip.

"Ms. Graham, let me be blunt." Lucian leaned back in his chair, studying her over his steepled fingers. "Any idiot can dig up pots. We didn't hire you to do manual labor. What we value is your insight, your intuition, and your ability to see patterns in random bits of historical data."

"Oh. Thank you." Very complimentary. But all she could hear was that she was losing her beloved project.

"How's your Dutch?"

"Excellent, sir." She'd studied all the languages of the European colonies in eastern America: Dutch, Spanish, Swedish, and French.

"Good. As of now, we're setting you up here in NYC. Your next project involves the early history of the Iroquois Confederacy here in New York State. New Amsterdam back then, of course. Hence, the need for Dutch."

Maya's lingering unhappiness swelled. "The history of the Haudenosaunee is well known."

"The who?"

"Haudenosaunee. It's what the Iroquois call themselves." He waved a hand, but she pressed on. "Their history is well documented. And, unlike the Ais and Mayaca, these Nations weren't destroyed. I really don't see how I could make a big difference…"

Fowler wasn't interested in her protests. "We've located previously unknown documents from the Dutch colonies which mention Iroquois sacred sites. We want you to locate those holy places."

That *would* be a boon to the modern tribes… and an interesting project… but Maya thought of Amesfield and couldn't muster much enthusiasm.

A fact that was not lost on Lucian. "Still not sold? Let me sweeten the deal. We'll bump your pay to $200,000 a year."

Her jaw dropped in a very unprofessional gape. "That's crazy! That's four times what I make now."

Pleased with her greed, Fowler smiled. A cool, predatory grin that stole a bit of her glee. "You deserve it. You deliver, where others have failed. We reward that."

Two *hundred* thousand. She'd never heard of an archeologist making that much! All of her protests died, killed by that insane number. "Sold!" she managed to croak…

Continue reading the next story in the Dragon Dreams series, Dragon Renegade, here on Amazon…

www.ingramcontent.com/pod-product-compliance
Lightning Source LLC
Chambersburg PA
CBHW030330160726
47992CB00005B/2220